Early

CW00850659

GINGER TH~~I~~

Also by Frank Kusy

Ginger the Buddha Cat

Rupee Millionaires

Kevin and I in India

All titles available from Grinning Bandit Books

Ginger the
Gangster Cat

Frank Kusy

First published in 2014 by

Grinning Bandit Books

http://grinningbandit.webnode.com

ISBN 978-0-9575851-5-7

DEDICATION

To Andi, my missus, and Sparky, my furry muse

Contents

Acknowledgements

Purrrrups! and thanks go to Sarah Monaghan, Terry Murphy and Cherry Gregory (for editing and laughs), Roman Laskowski (for web admin), Ted Cooper (for editing and 'oomans', lol), Anna Donovan (for my fab cover), and to all the good people on Authonomy who have helped with crits and comments. Prawwwwns all round!

Ginger the Gangster Cat

Prologue

Ginger was having a dream.

Not one of his usual dreams where he was killing things.

Nor the kind where he was maiming them first.

In this dream, he was the scourge of Victorian London.

Cunning and mean, the kingpin of a feline robber band, he was cocking one eye at the authorities and wearing a black silk patch over the other.

But the cat-nappers had finally caught up with him and he was being dragged off to pussy prison – there to rot for the rest of his horribly mis-spent life.

Now what was the name of the little precious who had grassed him up – Rafe? Rolf? Rufus? No matter, he would find that two-faced, turncoat kitten and make him pay.

And where was the rest of his gang – that mangy bunch of cowardly moggies who had fled to Spain? If it took him eight more lives, he would find them and make them pay too.

Chapter 1

Lost in the Woods

One misty, moisty morning, as Ginger was making his usual rounds, he came across a familiar black-and-white shape at the edge of the woods.

'Ere, I know you, don't I?' said big fat Ginger. 'Your name's Sparky, aint't it?'

Sparky sat sad and pathetic under a bush. He hadn't had a poo in two days and was missing his litter tray.

'Yes,' he said timidly. 'I think I'm lost.'

'You certainly are! I've seen your face on every tree in town. You're famous, you are!'

'I don't *feel* famous. I want to go home.'

'Don't we all?' sniffed Ginger, coming closer. 'I've been lost for ages, but you don't hear *me* complaining. I didn't get a poster like wot you did. And I certainly didn't get no celebrity write-up!'

'Why? What did it say?'

'Wot, the poster? 'Ow do I know? I don't read much ooman. But it filled up a whole page, and the photo was *great* - you look very nervous and far too soft for this world.'

Sparky hugged the edge of his bush, ready to retreat. He didn't know what to make of his unexpected orange guest.

'What *is* the world?' he asked shyly. 'Is it bigger than my kitchen?'

'My, my,' snorted Ginger, 'you *are* a babe in the woods, ain't you? And talking of woods, if it's good enough for a bear to poo in the woods, it's going to have to be good enough for you too. 'Ere, you look like you need to go...'

'No, I'm all right. I haven't eaten in two days.'

Ginger sized up his innocent prey. Should he put the frighteners on him, or let him in on his big plan? It was a tough call. He had his reputation to keep up, but what was he meant to do with such a pathetic looking creature? Scratching his ear, Ginger tried to think. Not much satisfaction chasing the young 'un down the street, was there? Not with him lost and frightened already. Still, there might be a way he could use it to his advantage...

'Two days?' he said at last. 'No wonder you look so thin. Look, I've got an idea. What say we both go to Barcelona? There's this lorry down the road wot takes me there and back every week. Trouble is, I'm so big and fat, nobody gives me any grub. But one look at you – all lean and feeble – and they'll be simply throwin' tapas treats

at you. That's the best thing about Spain. There's hardly any vegetarians!'

'What's a vegetarian?'

'You don't wanna know. That's why I left home. My owners fed me carrots. And sumfink called aubergines. Stoopid salad-crunchers!'

'So I shouldn't wait *here* then?'

'What for? I waited for my owners to claim me - after I decided carrots was better than nuffink – and then I got adopted by some mad old lady who kept talkin' at me all the time. Gawd, she could talk. I didn't get a minute's peace. Blah, blah, blah, she never shut up. And she made me watch soaps on TV every night, clamped to her lap, until I wanted to scream.'

'So I should go with you then?'

'Yeah, why not? You want to eat, don't you? And you're a young cat, with nine lives ahead of you. The world's your lobster!'

'Okay then,' sighed Sparky. 'Lead me to your lorry...'

*

At that moment, there was a high-pitched whistle, followed by an urgent cry of *'Sparky! Sparky!'*

'That's my human, Joe!' gasped Sparky excitedly. 'He's finally found me!'

'So Barcelona's off, then?' shrugged Ginger. And with a grunt of displeasure, he quietly slunk away.

Joe gasped with relief when he saw Sparky emerge,

small and miserable, from the undergrowth.

'*There* you are, baby cat!' he rejoiced. 'I've been looking for you everywhere. And here you are, lost in the woods. Did you jump over the end of our garden? Couldn't you get back? Have you been sitting here all this time? Golly, you must be hungry!'

And with that he whisked Sparky home in his van, put him back in his kitchen, and watched contentedly as his long-lost cat leapt into his litter tray and did the biggest poo of his young life.

*

Two whole days passed before Sparky left the kitchen again. And two more before he felt safe enough to venture back out into the garden.

There, to his surprise, he found Ginger waiting for him.

'I thought you were going to Barcelona?' he asked curiously.

'Yeah, I just got back,' said his friend. 'Why do you fink I'm wearing this "Kiss Me Kwik" sombrero? I had to nick it to keep off the sun.'

'And you're *still* wearing it? There's not much sun in Surrey.'

Ginger flipped the hat off with one paw, and pointed inside it with the other.

'You can fit a lot of food in a sombrero,' he announced proudly. 'Look 'ere – two dead seafood paellas and a chorizo sausage. You wanna try some?'

'Hmmm, smells *good!*" purred Sparky. 'But why are you being so nice to me?'

'I have my reasons,' said Ginger with a mysterious grin. 'One of them being I have no friends. I'm just one big ugly meanie – always have been – and all the other cats round here take one look at me and leg it. They don't appreciate my more sensitive side.

'*I'm* sensitive,' confessed Sparky. 'In fact, I'm *so* sensitive, I just can't kill anything. I think my owners are disappointed.'

'Disappointed? How come?'

'Well, I hear them talking, you know, and they think I'm a coward. I'm not sure what a coward is, but I don't think it's good.'

Ginger screwed up his nose in a sympathetic leer.

'That's the trubble with oomans,' he said. 'They expect you to bring 'em "presents" – usually small rubbishy ratty stuff and weeny birds – and then when you *do* bring 'em one, they go all horrified on you and make yer feel guilty. They want it both ways.'

'Have *you* killed anything?' asked Sparky timidly.

'Oh yerse,' said Ginger, reclining on the lawn. 'The very first fing I did for *my* oomans – the vegetarian ones – was catch a big fat rat in their shed and bite it in two right in front of them. Were they pleased? Were they heck! The first taste of real meat since I was born and they snatched it away and told me I was a murderer!'

'So I shouldn't kill anything then?'

'Nah, I didn't say *that*. You've got to show willing. And the word *do* get around. If other cats in the neighbour-hood have you down as a coward – a namby-pamby pussy with no...ahem...nuggets – they'll be in and out of your cat-flap, nickin' your food every day. You can't have *that!*'

'Well, I brought them a feather,' said Sparky feebly.

'A *feather?*' snorted Ginger. 'A bloomin' *feather?*'

'*Three* feathers, actually. I found them here in the garden.'

'And how did that go down?'

'Not very well, actually. Ol' Joe said, and I quote, "First a dead leaf, then a dead worm, then an almost-dead la-dybird, and now three dead feathers. Is he trying to prove something?" And Madge, my missus, said, "Four feathers is a sign of cowardice, isn't it, and Sparky can't even manage *that!*'

'Oomans!' grunted Ginger, wriggling on his back. 'I told you there was no pleasing 'em. It looks like you're gonna have to kill sumfink soon, or you'll be out on your ear.'

Sparky shivered miserably. He didn't want to go back under that bush. And he certainly didn't want other cats branding him a puff-ball and invading his cat flap.

'You may be right,' he confessed. 'Only yesterday, I

heard ol' Joe tell his missus he was going to find an elderly pigeon somewhere, tie it to a post, and wheel it out to the garden for me to lick to death. What can I do?'

'You don't have to do anything,' said Ginger, struggling to his feet. 'I said I was gonna help you, and I will. Though in return, you're going to have to help me. 'Ere, have a piece of this paella and I'll tell you my plan.'

As Sparky stuck his head into the upturned sombrero and savoured the delights of illegally imported Spanish cuisine, Ginger sloped off to the bottom of the garden and returned with something in his mouth.

'What's that?' enquired Sparky, the remains of a spicy sausage slowly dripping off his whiskers. 'A furry kind of leaf?'

'Are you serious?' snorted Ginger, dropping it to the ground. 'It's sumfink I killed earlier. It's a mouse.'

Sparky backed off nervously.

'That's a mouse? Why doesn't smell nice like the mouse in my kitchen?'

'That's because it's a *real* mouse, stoopid. Not some kind of catnip lookalike.'

'Won't it bite me or something?'

'No, I told you. It's dead, dead, dead. I should know. I played with it long enough. Then I buried it back there for a late-night snack.'

Sparky eyed Ginger warily. He was obviously mad.

'And you dug it up for what?'

Ginger the Gangster Cat

'I dug it up for *you*, you pampered pussy. You're goin' to pick up that mouse in that dainty little mouth of yours and take it in the house and pretend you killed it yourself.'

'Oh,' said Sparky innocently. 'Thank you...I think.'

'I know what's goin' on in that pretty little head,' smirked Ginger craftily. 'You're wondering what *I* get out of it. Well, like I told you before, I do have my reasons...'

*

'So did it work then?' asked Ginger the next day.

He was sitting high up on a fence, eager for news from his young protégé.

'Oh yes, indeed!' said a pleased Sparky. 'I dragged the mouse through the cat flap and sat next to it until my humans woke up. Joe was most impressed. He called me "good boy" and "brave little hunter" and made such a fuss of me that I felt like going out and killing my *own* mouse!'

'What about the uvver one, your missus?'

'Oh, she was more suspicious. I'd got bored of the mouse by the time she turned up and was licking my bum. She was even more suspicious when she put some cat food down and I tucked into that instead.'

"I bet that mouse was dead already!" she shouted up to Joe. "He's showing no interest in it at all!" So then I had to pretend that I hated processed cat food and began attacking the mouse.'

'And?'

'And that finally convinced her. "Urrrr!" she went. "I don't want mouse blood and guts all over my kitchen floor!" And then she put it in a plastic bag and chucked it in the bin. Good thing too, because it tasted *awful*."

'Nice one!' chortled Ginger happily. 'Now, about Barcelona...'

Chapter 2

The Cats who came in from the Cold

Sparky was a naive little cat, but he was not stupid. He knew he owed Ginger a favour, a *big* favour, but he had only just rediscovered his litter tray and he didn't want to leave it again for a *very* long time.

So he did what worked best with ol' Joe and his missus. He rolled over on his back – heedless of the cold patio stones - and went all cute and kittenish. Then he looked up at Ginger and asked, very politely, 'Are you hungry *now?'*

"Corse I'm hungry!' grumbled Ginger, clambering down from the fence. 'I gave you my last mouse yesterday, and I can't find anuvver one.'

'Well, what say you come in my cat flap and share what's in my bowl? It's always full, you know...'

'Full of *wot?'* jeered Ginger.

'Cat food. You know, what cats eat? Eight varieties. They're all good. Well, except "beef" of course. Ol' Joe tosses that one in the bin. He says cats don't eat cows."

'Well, he's not wrong there. But cat food, really? Jellified pieces of fish and meat with loads of chemicals in them? You call that cat food?'

'I've been watching TV,' said Sparky defensively. 'And one survey says that nine out of ten cats prefer it...'

'Yeah well, they *would*, wouldn't they? They're all *addicts*. They've been fed that muck since they was born. They don't know they've got a problem, they think they can handle it, but they can't. And I should know. They put weird gunk in those plastic packs wot keeps you coming back for more. That crazy ol' biddy wot adopted me kept feedin' me that rubbish until I doubled in size. And then I left her and went through a whole week of missin' it – crying like a baby I was and tearin' out clumps of my fur – until I caught a vole and got my taste for real meat back again!'

'Well,' said Sparky quietly, 'we've just eaten everything from Barcelona. And you – sorry, *we* – can't go back there for another week. So, unless you want to freeze to death on this cold and windy back lawn, you've got a choice. Cat food or nothing.'

Ginger eyed him warily. This little innocent might be young and raw, but he did have nerve. Either that or he was far too dumb for his own good. Whatever, he had just faced down the meanest, baddest, most ill-tempered cat in the neighbourhood (himself) – and had made him an offer he couldn't refuse.

Ginger the Gangster Cat

'Okay, cowboy,' he said with a sniff of respect. 'Let's check out the bowl situation...'

*

Joe was in the kitchen when he heard the cat-flap flick open.

'Hey, Sparky!' he called happily, 'have you brought another mouse?'

Well no, he noticed, Sparky had brought something else entirely. Something so large in fact, it couldn't get through the flap.

'Well, who's *this?"* said Joe. 'Have you brought a friend? My, he's a fat one, isn't he, and he doesn't look too comfortable!'

Ginger was mortified. He hoped no other cats were around, because he would lose his street cred forever. His head and the front half of his body had made it into the kitchen, but his swollen orange tummy – still heaving from recent Spanish repasts – had become solidly wedged in the open flap. He shot ol' Joe a look of pure hatred and wished himself dead.

Sparky grabbed hold of one of Ginger's ears – the one that was not half torn off – and tried to pull him in by it, but was met by pained squawks.

'No, don't do *that*, Sparky!' said Joe urgently. 'You'll just tear off the *other* ear. Let's push him back outside and I'll let him in through the back door.'

Ginger closed his eyes and suffered the ensuing indig-

13

nities in silence. Oomans. Whenever he got close to one, he always regretted it.

'I think I've got an extra bowl,' said Joe, ferreting around in the cluttered kitchen. 'Now, I've got you rabbit, Sparky, I know you like that. But what about your friend? He looks like a fish man!'

Ginger clocked the word 'crab' on the packet dangled in front of him, and recoiled in horror.

'I bloomin' *hate* fish!' he informed Sparky. Except prawns, of course. No yukky bones, and they don't fight back. Unlike that lousy lobster in the Barcelona fish market. I told it it was gonna die, lyin' there in that bucket of ice, but it didn't believe me and chopped half my ear off!'

Sparky didn't care. He was just grateful Joe hadn't kicked Ginger out. 'Look,' he said generously. 'You have the rabbit, and *I'll* have the fish, okay?'

It wasn't *entirely* okay with Ginger, but he was hungry. He ate with one eye on the bowl and the other on the long, gangling ooman who was – he felt certain – going to try and pick him up and fondle him some time real soon. Any ooman who had bent heaven and earth to find his precious little Sparky was obviously one of those touchy-feely cat-loving oomans who thought a tin of tuna automatically bought him a furry friend.

And Ginger was not wrong. The moment his bowl was empty, a pair of enormous hands came down and whisked him into the air.

'Bad move,' thought Ginger, and spat and hissed and cursed until he was let down again. Then, without further ado, he retreated backwards to the other end of the kitchen.

'Nice friends you have, Sparky,' said a disappointed Joe. 'And why is he walking *backwards?*'

'*Please* make an effort!' Sparky whispered across to Ginger. 'He's only trying to be friendly!'

'Yeah right,' growled back Ginger. 'Next thing I know, he'll be blah-blahing at me all day and makin' me watch bad spaghetti westerns.'

'Look, you helped me, and I'm trying to help you. It's only a week, after all, and then you'll be back in paella-land.'

Ginger sat at the back of the kitchen – fat, scruffy and disgruntled – and only came forward again when Joe reached inside his fridge and produced a bag of fresh prawns.

'Ow did he *know*?' thought Ginger wonderingly. 'I'm a *sucker* for fresh prawns! He's an evil genius, he is! But he's only gonna give me one - two at best. Then he's goin' to put 'em back in the fridge. How am I gonna get 'em *all*?'

Joe didn't know what hit him. He was just reaching down to tempt Ginger with a shiny pink prawn when a bright orange fireball leapt at his chest, grabbed the whole pack, and shot out of the kitchen and up the stairs. He was eventually located under Joe's Buddhist altar, gobbling down every single prawn and growling to himself with selfish pleasure.

Fortunately for him, Joe was very superstitious. Had Ginger chosen anywhere else in the house to indulge his gluttony, he would have been out on his ear. But under a Buddhist altar? Little did he know it, but Joe was quite crazy. He had long been convinced that Sparky was the reincarnation of his dear departed mother – a loving and good-natured soul who had died shortly before Sparky arrived. And now, by a similar crazy association (which had a lot to do with an overpowering passion for prawns) Joe decided that Ginger must be the reincarnation of his bad-tempered, food-mad, and emotionally damaged step-father Bert. He had never understood how his mother and Bert had lived together, let alone loved each other, but here they were again - he mused - two polar opposites, Sparky and Ginger, who just happened to be best friends.

'It's not his fault he's a mad, greedy piglet,' Joe told himself. 'He's just spent too long in the wild and doesn't know who he can trust. And if Sparky likes him, well, he can't be *all* bad - can he?'

But Joe was wrong. Ginger *was* all bad. He sat under the Buddhist altar all day, digesting his prawns, and then – simply because he felt like it – he came out and peed on the carpet.

'You can't do that!' said a worried Sparky, as Joe let out a howl of protest. 'Why don't you share my litter tray – that's what all *good* cats do!'

'No way,' retorted Ginger stiffly. 'I'm not sitting in your poo. And talking of poo, I feel a big 'un coming on, so he better let me outside – that stoopid ooman of yours – or I'll be dumpin' in his slippers.'

Sparky guided Joe to the garden door and uttered a shrill plaintive *prrrrrp!* It was his way of getting Joe to do anything he wanted. Seconds later, master and baby cat gazed on as Ginger scratched around on the newly-mown lawn round the back and laid a large sausage – as big as the one he had just brought back from Barcelona – right in the middle.

And all the time he was exerting himself, he was staring off into space as though it had nothing at all to do with him.

Sparky was appalled. So was Joe. His nice neat lawn was scratched and pooped on, and he only had minutes to sort it out before his wife returned from work. So he dashed inside, returned with some rubber gloves and a trowel, and furiously removed all evidence of Ginger's 'deposit'.

Madge's key turned in the lock the moment the offending sausage, now safely bagged up and odourless, dropped into Joe's bin.

'What kind of a day have you had, darling?' she enquired casually, and he said, 'Well, Sparky's found a new friend!'

'What *kind* of new friend?'

'A big fat orange one. Look, there he is out on the lawn, sniffing your rose bush.'

'*Sniffing* it?' howled Madge. 'He's *eating* it! That's *Dawn*, my favourite rose bush, and he's just chomped down all her blossoms!'

Ginger, hearing the commotion, stopped in his tracks and thought, 'Whoops. That must be the *other* ooman, the mad female one, and she don't look too happy.' So he threw up the rose blossoms, with a series of loud burps, and sat there waiting to be forgiven.

'He's not staying with us,' said Madge with finality. 'He's got to go.'

'But you're always saying Sparky needs a friend!' protested Joe. 'He's bored, you said, of toy mice and jingly little balls and could do with a proper playmate.'

'Yes, but not *this* guy. He's the spawn of Satan. See the way he's staring at me? If looks could kill, I'd be dead right now!'

Joe gave an involuntary shudder. He knew that black look. He didn't know where *from* exactly, but it made the hairs on the back of his neck stand on end.

Before he could say anything however, Sparky leapt to the defence of his new friend. 'Look,' he told Ginger ur-

Ginger the Gangster Cat

gently, 'I know that you're a master world-traveller – whatever "the world" is – but this is *my* world. So if you want me to come to Barcelona with you, you're going to have to behave yourself. First rule: roll over on your back and look cute. Second rule: don't upset my missus. She upsets really easily.'

Ginger gave a low sigh of resignation and rolled un-happily onto his back. He shot the female ooman a look of tired affection, and then licked the naked rose bush in a gesture of belated apology.

'See, I told you!' said Joe, secretly relieved. 'He's a good cat after all!'

Madge shrugged and went back in the house. 'It's your call,' she warned darkly. 'But I'm telling you, you're making a big mistake...'

Later on, as all four of them gathered for evening re-laxation in front of the 42- inch flat-screen TV, Sparky sat curled up on Joe's lap, heating up the fracture in his left leg, and Madge sat next to them, eyeing Ginger who sat bang in front of the screen looking miserable.

'Hmmm,' said Madge, 'I'm trying to watch an educa-tional film about juggling Romanian dwarves, and all that ginger monster wants to do is block my view and stare at me accusingly. What does he *want?*'

What Ginger wanted was to have his feet massaged. It was the only thing he had found oomans useful for. He waited until Sparky had overheated Joe's damaged leg and had been transferred to Madge, and then he trotted forward, dumped himself on Joe's lap, and stuck one of his paws in the air.

'Good lord!' exclaimed Joe as he found himself massaging the offered paw. 'He's actually *purring* !'

'Rather you than me,' sniffed Madge dismissively. 'Try touching him anywhere else and he just walks away backwards again.'

'Did you see him in the bath earlier?'

'I certainly did. That's the only other place he seems happy – sticking his head under the tap and sucking in the dribble of water coming out of it. All that time in the wild, he must be used to only drinking from drain-pipes.'

That wasn't *quite* the only place he seemed happy, thought Madge as she went to bed. He also liked following her into the toilet and purring under the bowl while she had a wee.

Chapter 3

Bloomin' Oomans

That night, curled up under Joe's Buddhist altar, and safe from probing ooman hands, Ginger lay wide awake.

He was suffering from a rare form of cat insomnia which made him afraid to go to sleep. He couldn't explain it – he hadn't bothered to either – but ever since he had moved in with Sparky, he was on full alert. All sorts of things were now swirling through his mind: losing Sparky, not making it to Barcelona, being banged up in a dark Victorian cell, dying of an empty tummy, the list just went on.

And it was getting worse. Now, he was convinced he was going blind. But only in the left eye, which he could not stop scratching. And who *were* those sixteen other cats who kept invading his thoughts? He wanted to scratch them too.

Ginger didn't like it, but with a long night ahead and nothing better to do, his eyes were starting to droop. And suddenly, without realising it, he was back in the land of Nod again, dreaming the dream he had tried to forget. And on this occasion, with crystal clarity, he recalled all eight of his previous lives upon this earth. From the very first one, where he had been worshipped as a (rather fat) god in ancient Egypt, through to his time as an (even fatter) lion in the arenas of Caesar's Rome, and then to his unfortunate blinding when a witches' 'familiar' in Protestant England. He had been too fat this time to escape the Inquisitors, and all sixteen of them had judged him guilty. His fourth life, he had been drowned at birth, and in the fifth, left to starve as the runt of a litter. Only in his sixth did he recover the use of one eye, though little good it did him, since he was surprised by an eagle on the arid plains of India and eaten alive. His seventh life, he had spent on a pirate ship - a galley-cat with an eye-patch, a wooden leg, and a strange fear of parrots. He had sailed the seven seas, and stolen his weight in gold, but then the rum had claimed him and he was lost overboard.

So at last he had glimpsed his eighth, and most recent, lifetime – in the seedy cut-throat backstreets of Dickens's London.

And oh dear, it wasn't rum that had ruined things this time – or even Rafe or Rufus.

It was Ralph.

Yes, he finally had the name.

And as the dream progressed, as this past life melded

into the present one, Ralph was no longer legging it to the cop-shop to grass him up.

Ralph was in fact no longer a small kitten, but a long hippyish ooman - complete with a tattered old head scarf, a pair of thick round glasses, and a busted left leg.

Worst of all, he was little Sparky's ooman and Ginger could not take his revenge. He wanted to (oh, did he want to!) but even as he yawned and slowly awoke, he knew that would be stupid. He was *this* close to gaining Sparky's trust – his meal ticket to Barcelona – and too much was at stake to rock the boat just yet.

Ginger looked around. This particular dream he remembered quite clearly, but nobody else could suspect.

*

In the next room, by a strange coincidence, Joe was having a dream of his own.

Unable to move, he was looking up at the dark pines.

He had been lost for days and his leg was hurting.

Something was chasing him – something large and orange.

A wood-mouse scurried past, but he was too weak to chase it.

As darkness fell, he knew he would never see home again and closed his eyes for the very last time.

Not long after, a fox came along and took advantage of a dead cat for a free meal.

But Ralph wasn't dead for long.

He was coming back.

And not as a cat.

*

Joe awoke with a start. Who was Ralph? And what was he was running away from? Most mysterious of all, why did he have one name in mind as he departed this world? *Alice.*

Joe put a lot of store by dreams. He had a 'Dictionary for Dreamers' which he had borrowed from a university bookshop 20 years before and which he had never returned. He had meant to, he really had, but he had never got round to it.

He looked up 'cats' and then 'fox' and then 'lost in woods', but came away none the wiser. All the book suggested was that he had a mysterious fear of foxes. Either that, or he had once been a cat – in a previous existence – and he hadn't liked it.

But it was not just dreams that fascinated Joe. He saw meaning in *everything.* In the buses he kept missing (bad bus karma), in the pointless life he was leading (bad reincarnation karma), and in the cats he kept losing and finding (bad and good cat karma).

He even saw meaning in the leg he had just broken. It was fate's way of telling him not to work anymore, he believed, and to spend his whole day on a futon watching endless re-runs of *Star Trek.* In fact, until Sparky came along, he had lost all interest in life.

Ginger the Gangster Cat

And now there was Ginger – the cat who obviously hated him, but who gave up his feet each evening for a massage. As soon as he had seen Ginger's 'black' look, he had stopped waiting to die. He felt pretty sure that Ginger would have 'helped' him along. There was something familiar about Ginger – *very* familiar – and though he had given him the benefit of the doubt earlier, his dream had changed everything.

Now, he did not trust him one inch.

*

Someone else who did not trust Ginger one inch was Madge, who had just returned from an aerobics class.

In her mind, Ginger was evil, pure evil. And Madge gave the benefit of the doubt to no-one. She only ever saw things in black and white, and was fond of shouting 'shut that *door!*' and 'close that *window!*' at total strangers.

When things were particularly black, to Joe's amusement, she lapsed into hysterics. The smallest things triggered her off - mainly loud noises and salivating people. Loud, salivating people were the most annoying of all.

'I was changing in the gym earlier,' she informed him, 'and these girls were going *thwack! thwack!* as they kept slamming the door, and they were chewing *gum* at the same time, which really got on my nerves. But what *really* got on my nerves was the girl at reception, who kept announcing over the tannoy: "We're closing now...the gym's closing in 10 minutes now...the gym's closing in 5 minutes now...the *facilities* are closing in 2 minutes now... it was like a blasted *countdown!* I felt like saying to her: "Someone needs to get home *really* urgently, don't they? I mean, we're not in a *military school,* are we? It's exactly what my father subjected me to - time pressure. I *hate* it!'

'Time pressure?'

'Yes,' Madge muttered darkly. 'All this makes me very *aggressive!*'

Joe briefly considered, and then put aside his kebab – which he was just about to salivate over.

'Look!' he beamed proudly. 'I'm not breathing!'

*

Later on that morning, Joe and Ginger confronted each other on the landing.

Ginger sat high up on a pile of freshly-ironed laundry, and as he squinted owlishly at Joe through his good right eye, his ooman nemesis – half-blinded by a recent laser operation - squinted owlishly back at him through his left. Rocked by recent revelations, these two would never see eye to eye again.

And as they heard Madge calling up 'Lunch!' from the kitchen, and the lengthy Mexican stand-off was finally broken, the partially-sighted pair were thinking the same thing: 'I know who you are, but do *you* know that *I* know?'

Ginger the Gangster Cat

The big difference was, Joe only *thought* he knew. Ginger was positive.

Chapter 4

Your Friendly Neighbourhood Ginger

The next day, after months of rain and dreary skies, the sun shone brightly and spring finally arrived. Madge flung open both garden doors and swarms of insect wild-life promptly invaded the breakfast room.

'Oh look, there's an ant-nest right by your feet!' she told Joe happily, and a cool breeze ushered in a large, inquisitive bee. Along with a couple of lost beetles and a cloud of newly-born flies. Sparky's eyes flitted back and forth, nervously surveying both the bee and the vast ex-panse of sprawling lawn full of creepy-crawly things. He waited until Joe began poking a gigantic spider with a stick, and then he fled upstairs to hide.

Where was Ginger, he wondered? He had last seen him in the kitchen, scouring the floor for stray prawns. And why wasn't he out in the garden, when it was such an obvious field-day for crunchy little bugs and insects?

The truth of it was, Ginger had repeated Sparky's trick and got himself lost. He had wandered out the front door behind Joe, as the ever-restless ooman nipped out to check his van battery, and then - since nobody had actually seen him vacate the house - he had been locked out and found himself abandoned in a street full of roaring cars and traffic.

'Ginger's gone,' said Joe three hours later. 'I can't find him anywhere...'

'Good riddance too,' mumbled Madge, nursing a big angry scratch on the back of her ankle. 'That nutter came at me out of nowhere this morning, and tore a lump out of my leg!'

'He must have thought it was mine,' suggested Joe. 'He hates me.'

'Yes well, I chased him downstairs with one of your crutches, and poked at him with it under your bed.'

'You did what?'

'I have to hand it to the old grump,' said Madge with a hint of admiration. 'He didn't show any fear at all – just batted away at the end of the crutch with both front paws and began fighting it!'

'Well, that explains it,' said Joe. 'No wonder he's gone!'

'And he's not coming back,' concluded Madge. 'He eats his weight in food, he takes up half the futon, he even gets his ruddy toes massaged. And what does he give back? Nothing! He's so spiky and unresponsive, unlike our sweet little Sparky who follows us everywhere. I'm *glad* he's gone. He was a real downer.'

As night drew in, and Madge retired to bed, she had occasion to eat her words. There was a strange little tip-tapping sound above her head, suggestive of a small rodent running back and forth, and she couldn't go to sleep.

'Where's Sparky?' she demanded crossly, getting out of bed and summoning Joe to her side. 'Here, hold this ladder, I'm going to shove him up into the attic and let him kill whatever's up there!'

Sparky was urgently *prrrrp*-ing by the front door, waiting for his humans to go out and look for Ginger, when he was rudely plucked into the air and thrust into a cold dark loft. He didn't know what he was doing there, but he knew he was not alone. There was something up there with him – something small and just as scared as he was.

'Hello!' he called out in the gloom. 'My name's Sparky – what's yours?'

A thin, desperate squeak echoed back from the farthest corner of the attic. It was Mister Squirrel, a little baby one, and although he didn't understand cat-speak he knew from the friendly tone that it wasn't dangerous. So he came out of his hidey-hole – very slowly, shivering with cold – and presented himself.

'Oh, you poor thing!' cried Sparky. 'You must be catching your death up here. Come on over here with me!'

Ginger the Gangster Cat

And so it was that, when Madge returned to the attic a long hour later and shone a light up into the attic, she saw Sparky sound asleep against the squirrel. The two of them had been cuddling up to each other for warmth.

'Well, this won't do!' she raged at Joe. 'I *told* you Sparky was a coward. He can't even kill a baby squirrel!'

'One day,' responded Joe calmly, 'Sparky will bring you a gerbil, or a robin, and you will be horrified as it gasps out its little life on your carpet. What do you want of him anyway? To be ultra-cute or a killer? You can't have *both!*'

'So what do you suggest?'

Joe considered. On the one hand, he was glad to be shot of Ginger – it was well past his bedtime – but on the other, if he didn't get him back, he wouldn't be going to bed at all.

'I suggest you go outside – like Sparky has been urging us to do all day – and find Ginger. I hate to say this, but he's the man for this job. Mister Squirrel won't have a chance.'

'And then I can sleep again?'

'Well, I can't get up the attic with my bad leg, and you – with your fear of blood and torture – wouldn't kill a fly!'

Grumbling under her breath, Madge snatched the torch, threw on some clothes, and went out into the street.

'*Ginger! Ginger!*' she called without much hope, and wandered down the road silently cursing to herself. It had begun raining again and as a light sheen of damp settled upon her tousled blonde hair, she hoped that none of the neighbours were watching. Particularly Ahmed, the dotty old Indian next door who fed all living creatures (even ants) but who strangely hated cats.

But she needn't have worried. Ginger had not gone far. If he had learnt one thing from Sparky, it was this: if you're a pussy with a good home, and you accidentally lose it, you don't run away. You stay put. Especially if it's raining and you want to be found again. So he had positioned himself under a bush, just three doors down from Joe's house, and as soon as he heard Madge's voice he dashed out to greet her.

'I don't like you,' Madge informed him. 'But I guess we both need each other. So let's get out of this rain and try and patch things up.'

Sparky was delighted to see his lost friend back again. He watched as Joe reluctantly dried Ginger off with a towel, and then he looked on - very gratefully - as Madge shoved him up into the attic. There was a surprised squawk of terror as Mister Squirrel departed this world, and then Ginger returned to the mouth of the loft, licking his lips and with cobwebs all around his mouth.

'I hope you didn't hurt him?' squeaked up Sparky.

'Good *boy!*' cried Joe and Madge in unison, and carried down Ginger in triumph.

Ginger wasn't used to being congratulated. For anything. And while his knowledge of ooman-speak was limited, he *did* know what 'good boy' meant. It was the opposite of '*bad* boy,' which meant he was about to be slapped around the head for pooping in someone's hat or tearing up their curtains. '*Good* boy,' which he had only ever heard applied to Sparky, was generally followed by a trip to the fridge and a big reward.

It was a new sensation, being the hero of the hour, and as Ginger tucked into his bowl of hand-selected Atlantic prawns, he set aside his dark hatred of oomans for a moment. 'Well, at least I'm good for *sumfink!*" he thought grudgingly. 'If I'd known they liked dead fings, I could have been "good boy" a lot sooner!'

But Ginger was a slow learner. He was an old cat, not up for new tricks, and besides, he still had his heart set on returning to Barcelona.

'Whaddya mean "good boy" isn't "good boy" in Spanish?' he quizzed Sparky later. 'What *is* it then?'

It was late in the day, and the two cats were sitting at a large bay-window at the top of house – watching the pigeons fly up and the sun go down.

'Humans aren't like us,' said Sparky hesitantly. 'They live in different countries, apparently, and they speak different languages. I only know this because we have a Spanish maid. She comes to clean the house each week, and she calls me *buen chico*.'

'Boo-wen cheeko?' mocked Ginger. 'Well, la-de-dah!'

'You're not taking this very seriously,' said Sparky. 'Do you want to learn or not?'

'As long as it's not bloomin' *Spanish*. And 'ow come you know so much ooman-speak anyway? It ain't natural.'

'It is in *my* house,' said Sparky proudly. 'Six months with *my* humans and *anyone* would understand English. They talk to each other non-stop, and to me in particular.'

'That don't mean nothing,' said Ginger, dreaming of pigeon pie. 'My old lady blah-blahed at me every day and I was still none the wiser.'

'Well,' paused Sparky, 'I *was*. The first word I learnt, naturally enough, was "bowl". Then came "food", "fridge", and "litter tray". After that – and I really don't know how this happened – *everything* my humans said started to make sense. It's almost as though as I *was* human!''

'You wot?'

'Well, they weren't talking *at* me anymore. They were talking *to* me, and I understood.'

Ginger eyed him with a mixture of awe and suspicion. Up until a couple of days ago, he had made *not* talking to anyone, let alone listening to them, his stock in trade. His motto then had been simple: 'If it's small and squeaking, eat it. If it's big and barking, get up a tree.' The thought of actually engaging any other creature in conversation – apart from Sparky – had never entered his mind.

Along with this thought came another. That if Sparky could learn English ooman-speak so quickly, he could pick up the Spanish version just as fast. And that, in Ginger's book, made him a walking, talking gold mine. 'Cor!' he thought enthusiastically, 'I could really *use* him! Forget about the "sad and pathetic pussy" routine. I could park him outside any Barcelona cafe or tapas bar, and he'd know *exactly* when oomans was totally stuffed and up for givin' away their leftovers!'

*

The Spanish maid, Juanita, turned up on Wednesday. She was young and pretty, and she had even less English than Ginger. Which suited him just fine, because he wanted Sparky to learn Spanish. But there was just one problem. Juanita came with a hoover, and the moment she turned it on, Sparky leapt up with fright and vacated the premises. He was very sensitive to loud noises and hoovers were number one on his list of things to run away from.

'Come back, you nervous little pussy!' Ginger called after him, but Sparky had already cleared the garden and was shivering behind the shed. He was only persuaded back in again when Ginger tugged the hoover lead out of its socket and left Juanita without a power source. And to make quite sure she couldn't plug it in again, he sprayed on the socket and turned it into a damp electrical hazard.

'*Mierda!*' cried Juanita as she carted the hoover upstairs and found all the other sockets similarly sabotaged. '*Gato estupido!*'

'I think she said "blimey" and called me a "stoopid cat!"' chortled Ginger happily. 'We can *use* that...'

'*Pooh!*' said a disgusted Sparky. 'You've just stunk out the whole house."

'*Totally* worth it, man! We've just learnt our first three words of Spanish!'

But Ginger's triumph was short-lived. Juanita stopped just long enough to deodorise the plug sockets and to throw open all the windows, and then she upped and left. Without even leaving a note.

'That's strange,' commented Joe on their return. 'The whole place smells of bleach and there's a force nine gale blowing through it. Has Juanita lost her mind?'

'Hmmm,' said Madge, sniffing the air, 'I think we've lost *Juanita.* Look, there's the hoover standing idle in the hall, and there's something *behind* the bleach that reeks of *cat pee.* Where's that blasted Ginger?

Ginger was wisely out of sight, licking his bum behind the garden shed. He was planning on how to get back in the house without becoming a 'bad boy' again. Somebody else would have to take the fall for his crime, and it couldn't be him or Sparky. So, after due deliberation, he broke his long vow of silence with other cats, and struck up a conversation with a big black one called Valentino, who just happened to be passing by.

'Ere, mate,' he growled sweetly. 'No, don't run away. I just wanna word with you.'

'You don't call *anyone* "mate", said Valentino cagily. 'You're going to bite me or something, aren't you?'

'Nah, I wouldn't do that. I just wanna do you a favour. See that house down there? Well, it's got a cat-flap, and if you go in it, you'll find this gorgeous little tabby wot's dying for a boyfriend. She tried it on with me earlier but, as you can see, I'm a fat old blob wot can't please the ladies no more. *You*, on the other hand – a dashing young feller like *you* - well, you'd have no trouble. She'd be lickin' her lips the moment she clapped eyes on *you!*"

'Really?' said Valentino – who quite fancied himself as the local ladies' man – and he galloped gullibly down the garden and through the open flap. Seconds later, he was back out again and being chased up the lawn by an irate Madge with a broom.

'Spray our house out, will you?' she shouted after him. 'You're a very naughty dirty cat, and if my husband sees you again he's going to shoot you with his air pistol!'

'You *rotter* !' puffed Valentino as he passed Ginger. 'You totally set me up!'

'Sucker!' smirked Ginger with a satisfied grin and

slowly sloped back down into the house.

Here he found Sparky, who was doing what he always did when he wanted some 'alone' time. He was sitting on his favourite stool next to the very warmest radiator, kneading an old woollen poncho from India with his two front paws and dribbling into it with sheer pleasure. It was warm and furry, and it reminded him of his mother's tummy when he was just a tiny suckling new-born.

Looking at him, Ginger was overcome by a wave of unusual sentiment. He had never had any kittens - well, none he had stuck around long enough to look after anyway - and he was filled with an annoying feeling of gluey fondness. It annoyed him because he had never been fond of *anything* before, and it made him feel weak, like a cissy-cat with no claws.

'What am I doin'?' he found himself thinking. 'Draggin' this poor little innocent to Barcelona, makin' him learn Spanish, even sprayin' out his house! If I took one eye off him in the big wide world, he'd be eaten alive!'

But then he pulled himself together. He was a big bad killing machine, a cat to be reckoned with, and he wasn't about to go soft on anyone. Even when that 'anyone' was Sparky – the cutest and most cuddly kitten in the universe. He would just have to toughen him up, that's all, and that was when Ginger thought of Ben.

*

Ben was the largest, loudest and dumbest dog in the

neighbourhood. He lived three doors down, at number 25, and he had 'I hate cats' written all over him. He was bored senseless of being kept indoors all day, and on the rare occasion he was let out for walkies he would break leash at the sight of a cat and run for miles to catch it.

Ginger had had lots of fun with Ben – leading him on wild-goose chases up and down the road, then hiding up trees, just out of reach, as the huge, slavering Labrador senselessly barked its head off in frustrated rage. And now he thought Sparky deserved a bit of fun too.

'We're goin' on a little adventure,' he said as Sparky finished pawing his damp poncho. 'It's time you met a dog.'

'A dog? What's that?'

'That's an animal you run away from. Yes, I know you run away from everyfink, but this is different. Dogs is like a *game*. They is big and loud, but also very slow and stoopid. The idea is, you wander past them, making like you haven't seen 'em, and then you leg it up a tree or a fence and pull funny faces at them. It drives 'em *crazy!*"

'Do we have to?' said Sparky timidly. 'It sounds rather dangerous...'

Ginger gave a sigh of despair. It was no good telling his nervous disciple that dogs *were* dangerous, that they would tear him into tiny pieces if they caught him. He would have to try a different tack.

'*Dangerous?* Nah! They love it, they do. Dogs was

born to chase cats, and it gives 'em a lot more exercise than just wanderin' down roads and peein' against lamp-posts. Besides, if you are slow and they do catch you, all they do is give you a jolly good *licking.'*

'Do I want to be licked by a dog?'

'No, not really,' said Ginger carefully. 'They smells sumfink grim. That's the problem with dogs. They is not hygienic.'

'They don't clean themselves?' said Sparky, horrified.

'Nah, they let their oomans do that *for* them, lazy lummoxes. Why do you fink we run away from them? They stink to high heaven.'

'Oh, the poor unwashed creatures!' sympathised Sparky. 'Do you really want me to meet one?'

'Yeah, why not? If you leave any more cat saliva on that blanket of yours, it'll be standing up on its own!'

Ben was hard at work, gnawing on a meat-flavoured rubber bone, when Ginger and Sparky turned up. Ginger tapped on the thin garden window separating dog from cat and waved a cheery 'hello!' Then he sat back and awaited the inevitable response. Ben clambered awk-wardly to his feet, tossed aside the useless bone, and crashed against the double-glazed glass until it shivered on its mountings. He couldn't believe the sheer *gall* of these two cats – one big and bolshy, the other small and sleepy – who were sitting literally inches away from his slobbering jaws. He wanted to kill them both very badly.

Ginger the Gangster Cat

'Oh,' said Ben's owner, conveniently opening the garden door, 'there's that horrible orange cat who keeps pooping on our lawn. Go on, Ben – see him off!'

And with a howl of joy, Ben launched himself out into the open and stupidly went after Ginger. He could have had Sparky, who was rather looking forward to being licked by a dog and who hadn't moved an inch, but he didn't. Ben liked things to *move* when he chased them, and Ginger moved very fast – dodging in and out of flower-pots and hedges, and causing absolute mayhem. By the time Ginger was finished with him, Ben had clumsily trodden down or uprooted nearly every budding plant or bush in the garden.

It was not a good day for Ben. Not only had he failed to catch Ginger – who had now found safe haven on the shed roof – but his owner John had unexpectedly taken to Sparky and he wasn't allowed to molest him either.

'Leave him *alone,* Ben!' ordered John. 'He's only a poor little baby cat, and you're just making him nervous. For heaven's sake, stop *barking!*"

Ginger couldn't believe his eyes. Here he was sitting high up on a roof, and there was Sparky way down below, being fussed over by his least favourite ooman and his least favourite dog. 'Blimey!' he muttered to himself. 'He's even got the bloomin' dog *licking* him. And he's *liking* it! There's something not quite right 'ere!'

But Sparky couldn't see the problem. In his mind, he

41

had just made two new friends. Yes, one of them had very bad breath and a tongue like sandpaper, but they both seemed to like him. So much so indeed, that he was invited inside and given a whole pot of real tinned tuna. Then John picked him up and carried him gently back home again.

'I like dogs,' Sparky informed a disbelieving Ginger later. 'All they need is a little mouthwash.'

Ginger promptly put Barcelona on hold.

Chapter 5

The Loss of Innocence

The following week, Ginger discovered the power of flight. One second his head was buried in Madge's breakfast bowl, slurping down porridge-milk like there was no tomorrow; the next, he was airborne and sailing down the garden like a fat, furry zeppelin.

'I can *fly!* I can *fly!*'' he thought as he high-fived a passing pigeon, and then 'no, I *can't!*' as he nosedived into the pond. 'G*aargh!*' he spluttered, 'what's wiv all this water? I can't *swim!*''

Joe leaned tiredly over Madge's shoulder and said 'What's he done now?'

'He's helped himself to my *porridge!*''

'And so you threw him into the pond? Wasn't that a bit drastic?'

'Well, he's got to learn,' Madge shrugged. 'He's a mean tangerine eating machine!'

Ginger struggled out of the pond like the creature from the black lagoon. He was covered in green slime and in the mood for murder. Once again, his street cred had been seriously damaged, and all over a bowl of *milk* for Gawd's sake! He shot Madge a look of damp hatred and silently vowed his revenge.

Sometime later, he found Sparky playing with a toad. It was a small toad, just past being a tadpole, and Sparky had adopted it. He had one front paw on it, to stop it jumping away, and he was chatting away to it as though it was a long-lost relative.

'Hello, Mister Toad!' said Sparky. 'I like you lots because every time I touch you, you go *ribbit! ribbit!* and grin back at me. Will you be my new friend?'

Ginger looked on with annoyance. Why was Sparky so bloomin' happy? And why was he always the 'good boy' and never punished? It just wasn't fair. And so, still dripping with pond scum and still filled with spite, he decided to stitch Sparky up. He wanted to punish Joe too (well, 'Ralph' *did* have it coming!) but he still needed Sparky, and Sparky needed Joe. So he did the next best thing, and picked on Joe's missus instead. She also had it coming.

He ran in the house, bit the back of Madge's ankle again, and hid away as she exploded into the garden, looking for her attacker.

But she found only one cat there.

'*Sparky?*' she spluttered angrily. 'Well, I can't believe it – you're picking up bad tricks, aren't you? And what's that you've got there? A toad? A bad cat like you doesn't deserve a toad. Give it here!'

And in a fit of pique, she picked up the toad, tossed it over the fence, and stormed back into the house.

Sparky stared bemused at the empty piece of grass. 'That was my *toad!*' he cried piteously. 'He was my friend, he was, and you've just thrown him *away!*'

Ginger felt bad at framing Sparky, but it had to be done. Not only had he got even with the nasty female ooman – ah, vengeance was *sweet* – but he had also got rid of that darned toad. He hadn't liked that toad. Sparky had been getting far too fond of it.

Something else Sparky had been getting far too fond of was chicken roll. The problem had started a few days before, when Joe brought home two packs of the stuff and Madge had used them to teach Sparky a new trick. Bending down slowly, with one slice of chicken roll dangling enticingly from her teeth, she had somehow got the cat to levitate on its back legs – front limbs plastered to its sides like a penguin – and to eat the meat in midair.

Since then, Sparky had touched nothing else. He turned his back on even the choicest cat food and preferred to starve rather than eat from his bowl. Joe had tried being patient with him, showing him the empty fridge and telling him that he really must break this nasty habit, but then Sparky had fixed him with such a pitiful stare that he had found himself limping back to Tesco's to buy more of the stuff.

'How many slices of chicken roll has he had today?' Joe had asked Madge, and when she said 'fifteen' he'd rolled his eyes and said 'that cat has a serious problem.'

Even Ginger was concerned, because now that Sparky had been blamed for his rash attack on Madge, she had closed the fridge door on her ex-favourite pussy and cut him off from his daily 'fix' of chicken roll. She didn't like to do it – it had taken her *hours* to perfect that wonderful circus trick – but (sigh) he had to learn his lesson.

'It's like the Devil's catnip, that chicken roll!' marvelled Joe later on. 'Look, he's a slave to it! All the signs are there – uncontrollable shivering, restless pacing of the kitchen, and desperate sniffing of the fridge door. I should report you to the RSPCA for hooking him on the stuff!'

'How was I to know?' wailed Madge. 'It's no mean feat, you know, teaching a cat to eat chicken-roll from your mouth without him scratching your eyes out!'

'Well, we'll have to be cruel to be kind. Don't give him anymore!'

But Sparky without chicken roll was like a cat consigned to Hell. He either faced the wall, staring dismally into the void, or he walked off to sulk in the garden. When all else failed, he sat heavily on Madge's computer (while she was still using it) and erased a whole day's work.

It was a long, long week before he came out of his depression. He could not understand why his owners were being so cruel, when he had done nothing to deserve it, and his faith in human-kind sank to zero.

In the end, Ginger couldn't bear it any longer and came clean. He crept up on Madge, bit her on exactly the same spot as he had before, and then just sat back – eyes closed – to await her retribution.

'Oh, so it was *you*, was it?' Madge shouted at him. 'I should have known. And all this time we've been punishing poor little Sparky!'

'Don't be too hard on him, darling,' said Joe soothingly. 'Just think – he probably saved Sparky's life.'

'How do you mean?'

'Well, Sparky was practically climbing the walls. A few more days and he would have jumped off the roof!'

Madge had to admit he was right, but she wasn't happy about it. Sparky had been so seriously distressed by his recent experiences, he was no longer the same cat. He no longer ran up to greet her when she opened the door, he no longer purred in her arms, he didn't even wanted to be picked up. He was a pussy in peril.

And so Joe called in a cat counsellor. It was a desperate measure, but it worked. An elderly lady by the name of Edna came around and talked to Sparky for a whole hour. She had no cats of her own – since she lived in a council flat that allowed none – but she did have nineteen toy ones made of rags and wool, and she talked to *them* all the time. She told Sparky that he was a *good* boy, that his owners hadn't meant to make him sad, and that they were deeply sorry. She said that even humans make mistakes, and that they would do *anything* – short of giving him more chicken roll – to make him happy again.

'Look,' she said in the end, 'they love you more than anything in the world, and if you don't love them back, they will cry and cry and cry. Besides, who was it who came and found you when you were lost in the woods? *Who* was it? And *where* would you be if they hadn't?'

'In Barcelona!' thought Ginger sourly. But even he was impressed by this pretty little speech. And he, more than anyone, wanted the old Sparky back. The new one was downright depressing.

At the end of the hour, Sparky lifted his forlorn head and decided that life was good again. All this time, he had been blaming others when he should have been blaming himself. He knew that his innocence was shot, that he would always have this weakness, but he swore off chicken roll forever. And he forgave those responsible for leading him to it – Joe and Madge – and even Ginger for making him quit.

'Thank heaven!' they all rejoiced as Edna finished her trance-like little chat. 'He's *purring* again! Get him his favourite poncho!'

And as Sparky settled back into his warm woolly blanket, and began dribbling contentedly into it, the household breathed a collective sigh of relief. At number 28, Causton Road, all was well once more.

*

Or was it?

Still in the thrall of Edna's hypnotic drone, Sparky's paws began to twitch and quiver.

He was falling asleep, and he was starting to dream.

And in this dream he was looking up at the sky, unable to move.

Something bad had happened, and every bone in his body was hurting.

He was lying in the road and – far off in the distance it seemed – some ghostly voice was shouting *'Alice! Alice!'*

'Who's Alice?' he wondered dimly and slowly closed his eyes.

It was an awful dream, more of a nightmare really, and as Sparky's 'inner kitten' kicked in again, he quickly replaced it with dreams of a much more pleasant kind – dreams of his toad.

Chapter 6

The Great Escape

Joe's leg was getting better. So much so, that he managed to hobble up to the garden shed and retrieve two dusty cat-boxes. The first signs of summer had signalled the first wave of fleas, and both cats were infested with them. Joe knew this because fleas were very partial to Madge, and both her legs were covered in painful bites.

'You've got nothing *else* to do all day!' she lectured him. 'You can at least help me get those cats down to the vets!'

Ginger watched Joe limp back into the house with alarm. He knew a cat box when he saw one, and he knew what generally happened afterwards.

'*Scarper!*'' he alerted a sleepy Sparky. 'Get *out* of 'ere!'

'What?' said Sparky with a yawn. 'I was just dreaming of my toad, and he was telling me all sorts of nice stories!'

'Blow your toad! They're takin' us down the *vets!*''

Ginger the Gangster Cat

'What's a vet?'

'A vet is some vile ooman wot sticks a cold tube up your bum. I should know, I've seen enough of 'em. And that's not the worst of it. They've got a big needle and shoves it in your neck! I would say it "ain't ooman", but it is! They're the most horrible oomans of all!'

But before they had time to act, Joe had locked them in the back room and dropped them, wildly protesting, into two little cages. Then he swung out into the street, lurching on his bad leg, and took them on a trip to hell. Madge followed on behind, urgently talking to them and telling them what good boys they were.

'Good boys, my eye!' Ginger called across to Sparky. 'She just don't want a couple of flea-bags in her house! I bloomin' *hate* oomans!'

Sparky was terrified. Ginger's lecture had put the fear of God into him. Six months had passed since his first trip to the vets, when he was just a tiny kitten in need of in-oculations, and he had blocked out the event completely. All he knew now was that he was being carried down the road, past screeching cars and lorries, to some kind of torture chamber. And if to confirm this, Joe started *singing* at him, which sounded like a bagful of cats in pain and sent shivers up and down his spine.

The veterinarian on duty that day was a no-nonsense nurse called Grace, a blonde Australian with a blunt sense of humour.

Frank Kusy

'Well, let's get *this* little feller out first!' she gestured at Sparky, 'He's so *cute*, I could just eat him up!'

Sparky crept out of his box with fearful anticipation. Did she really want him for lunch?

No, she had something far worse in mind. Before he had time to blink, she had placed him on a high bench, lifted his perky little tail, and shoved an ice-cold thermometer up his bum.

'Might as well check him for fever while we're at it!' stated Grace cheerfully.

Madge, who was stroking his head to keep him calm, was in the wrong place at the wrong time. Without warning, a startled Sparky clamped himself onto her ample bosom and tried to climb up it.

The sounds of tearing flesh and wailing cat were hard to separate.

'Busy little feller, ain't he?' grunted Grace carelessly. 'I guess I shoulda cut his claws first!'

'You *think* so?' howled Madge as blood ran down her chest. 'I look like the victim of a slasher movie!'

'It's not that bad, darling!' said Joe, desperately dabbing her with antiseptic ointment. 'The worst is over!'

But it wasn't. With Sparky safely jabbed and tabbed and stuck back in his box, it was Ginger's turn.

'Well, he's a big 'un!' announced Grace with some surprise. 'How the heck did you get him in that tiny cage?'

Ginger the Gangster Cat

What she should have asked was how they were going to get Ginger *out* of the cage. They tried everything – pleading, cajoling, even tempting him with tasty treats, but he remained defiant at the back of the box. Grace unwisely put her hands inside to pull him out but he just hissed at her and bit two of her fingers.

'Ow, you crazy fat toe-rag!' she shrieked, and lifted the box high in the air to shake him out. But he wasn't coming. He clung to the side grid like a trapeze artist, swinging heavily back and forth, and he only let go to bounce off the inspection bench. Then he hid behind the weighing scales, swearing like a mad thing.

'I don't *want* a botty probe!' he spat hysterically at them. 'If you come any closer, I'm going next door and taking a puppy hostage!'

In the end, of course, he had to succumb. Three large pairs of ooman hands approaching him from different directions left him trussed up in a towelled strait-jacket, with a worming tablet shoved down his throat and something much colder plunged up his nether regions.

'Cor!' he announced miserably as they were taken back home again. 'My bum don't half hurt. What about yours?'

Sparky did not answer. He had just been violated, and he did not want to talk about it ever again.

*

Things went quiet for a while after that.

Frank Kusy

As spring turned into summer, Sparky and Ginger spent most of their time in the garden, which they had now divided into two strips of territory. Sparky, growing bolder by the day, now controlled the front half of the lawn – where he could bat away small flies, moths and minor flying things – while Ginger took pole position on the top of the garden shed and chased away squirrels, rats and interloping cats. It was a good arrangement, one which required Sparky to kill absolutely nothing and Ginger to indulge his blood-lust to the full. On occasion, because he knew he was supposed to, he brought in a dead rodent or two, which Joe or Madge routinely bagged up and put in the bin. On other occasions, he dragged in something bigger – an annoying pigeon perhaps – just to show he could go the extra mile.

Madge was particularly happy about the pigeons. She had a long-standing feud with Ahmed at number 27, who fancied himself as a latter-day Francis of Assisi. Ever since he'd lost his wife a few years before, he had begun feeding things, particularly birds. He had started his Franciscan mission by feeding the swans down by the Thames – in full view of the sign saying "Do Not Feed the Birds." When chastised by the council, he had moved closer to home and begun feeding the pigeons under the nearby railway bridge, but the council hadn't liked this either. They received so many complaints from pooped-on passers-by that they slapped an ASBO on him. Since then, he had restricted his Mary Poppins activities to the confines of his own back garden. Every day, squadrons of seagulls, crows, and other fluttering birdlife would now descend on his extension roof – where he flung handfuls of dried bread and biscuits – and their loud piercing shrieks drove poor Madge crazy.

'It's like a scene from *The Birds!*' she complained bitterly. 'There's so many of them now, they've started crashing into my window while I'm trying to read. Why can't he feed them at the *bottom* of the garden instead of the top?'

The answer was simple. Ahmed had learnt that Ginger lived at the bottom of the garden.

So had all the pigeons, none of whom dared land there anymore.

'Allah say all creature are one,' declared Ahmed stubbornly. 'And all creature need the *food!*'

'Well, why don't you feed our *cat?*' reasoned Joe, pointing at winsome little Sparky. 'I've just been on the internet and Muhammed was apparently so fond of cats that he cut off his own sleeve rather than disturb one of them.'

But Ahmed wasn't interested. All he knew was that his beloved flying friends were being slaughtered on a daily basis.

'*This* is your cat also?' he said accusingly, stabbing a gnarled finger towards Ginger.

'No,' lied Madge glibly, 'he just likes it up there. Though if you keep feeding those damn birds by my window, I can adopt him and bring him down *here*. After all, *he* is a "living creature" and he "need the food" too.'

Ahmed didn't like her logic, but he couldn't dispute it. With great reluctance, he put the bird-crumbs away.

But Madge was not quite done with him yet. Ahmed's best friend was his 'lady fox' who lived round the back of Wickes' hardware store down the road. A couple of nights later, around 11pm, Madge saw him sneak off in his battered old sandals (and one of his weird furry hats) to feed her. He was gingerly holding a plate with human food on it, and she confronted him, saying, 'We don't want you feeding that fox, because we have a baby cat and it might come around and eat it.' Well, Ahmed didn't like that at all. 'You no want good neighbour *relations?*' he shouted and stormed off.

Five minutes later, realising that he might have overstepped the mark, he returned to bang insistently on her front door. When Madge eventually opened it, he shoved a plate of one cut-up banana in her face and said, 'Banana! *Good* ! *Sweet* !' And then, 'I am very interested in children! You make some, I look after them!' Which roughly translated as: 'If you have kids of your own, you wouldn't fuss so much over that ruddy cat!'

*

Madge was becoming concerned.

Ginger the Gangster Cat

Of late, ever since Ginger had arrived, Joe had been exhibiting the strangest behaviour. Not only had he begun twirling the ends of his moustache into the semblance of whiskers (and pawing his face with wet fingers), but he had let his nails grow to feral proportions and was experimentally raking the futon with them. Most disturbing of all, he had started uttering cat-like grunts of pleasure when presented with his food, and was often to be found lurking by the fridge, waiting for treats.

Before Joe went *too* far and started using Sparky's litter tray, Madge took action. It was now the end of May, and she turned his attention to planning his annual birthday holiday. Every year, in June, she took him somewhere different in Europe — Budapest, Vienna, Gdansk, Prague — just to get away from sweltering Surrey. Okay, it was sweltering everywhere *else* in June, but at least the hotels had air-conditioning.

'What about Barcelona?' she suggested out of the blue, and Ginger's ears instantly pricked up. It was one of the few ooman words he knew well, and he was overcome by his old wanderlust.

'*Barcelona*?' he thought disbelievingly. 'Did I hear her right?'

'Barcelona?' yawned Joe without much interest. 'What's there then?'

'Well, there's a wonderful mixture of culture and

beautiful architecture – like the Gaudi museum – and loads of interesting street-life, with cafes and bars. You'll love it!'

'Will I? Well, okay then, I'll check out hotels on the net. Do they have air-conditioning?'

'Of course they do!'

'Because you remember that time we went to Seville in June. It was fifty degrees in the shade, and even my sunglasses were melting.'

'That was *interior* Spain,' argued Madge convincingly. 'Barcelona is on the coast, with lots of breezy sea air. And besides, *I've* always wanted to go there.'

'Well, why didn't you say so? I'll get on it right away...'

But then Joe paused and thought.

'Hang on,' he said. 'What about the cats? We could have farmed out Sparky to the vets for a week or two, but they'll never take Ginger. Not after what *he* did...'

'How's about a cat's holiday home?' suggested Madge. 'I've heard of a real good one in Faversham. I think it's called Katz Castle.'

Ginger had also heard of Katz Castle, but the very mention of these two words made his heart sink. His original owner, a ghastly child who had only wanted a cat for Christmas and not even for the New Year, had abandoned him there years before and left him to rot. It had been months before his next owners – the die-hard vegetarians – had turned up, and by that time his faith in human nature was crushed. He had in fact become so mean and vicious that he had begun terrorising all the other cats and had been relegated to an isolation cell. He well remembered the cruel owner of the 'holiday home,' Annie, who had warned the vegetarians that he was 'still not ready to be presented.' And then the supreme effort of will he'd had to make to convince them, with fake purring and rubbing of noses, that he was a reformed cat, worthy of a new home. He would have done *anything*, by this point, to get out of that hellhole.

'Do you want the good news or the bad news?' he informed Sparky shortly.

Sparky shot him a worried look.

'The *good* news,' continued Ginger, 'is that your oomans are going to Barcelona. Yes, my favourite destination. The *bad* news is that they ain't taking us with them.'

'Oh,' said Sparky sadly, 'why's that then?'

'They has to go there in a big flying fing called an aeroplane. And cats is not allowed on it because some oomans hate cats and just won't sit with them.'

'So what do we do? Do we stay in the kitchen?'

'No,' said Ginger craftily. 'We is going to Barcelona *too*. Unless of course you'd rather stay at a horrible cat home with shared litter trays and no garden to play in.'

'Is that where they're taking us?' shivered Sparky. 'Don't they love us anymore?'

'They ain't got no choice. They needs a holiday, and they can't leave a baby cat like you alone for two weeks.'

'Can't *you* look after me?'

'Nah, come off it. They wouldn't trust me with a gold-fish.'

'So where's the "good" news, then? It sounds all bad to *me*.'

'Don't worry your pretty little head about it,' smirked Ginger confidently. 'I've got a cunning plan...'

Ginger's plan drew heavily on the British World War Two films he had been forced to watch with Joe on the futon. It was the price he had had to pay for having his feet massaged nightly. Joe was particularly fond of 'escape' movies where sad oomans - trapped in prisons just like Katz Castle – dug tunnels, forged passports, learnt something called German, and legged it back home dressed as Norwegian sailors.

He knew he would have to return to Katz Castle – there was no getting around that – but once inside he (and Sparky) would have to escape immediately. Any delay and Barcelona would be off. The key thing, the one essential ingredient of his plan, was that they not get separated. Somehow, he would have to arrange it so that Annie, or whoever now ran the home, put the two of them in the same cage.

It was the 12th of June when the cat-boxes reappeared from the shed. Though this time, curiously, neither Ginger nor Sparky put up a fight. They both stepped into the boxes, waited patiently until the front grids were latched on, and let themselves be carried into Joe's waiting van without a murmur.

'That's very strange,' said Madge. 'Did you drug them or something?'

'I was wondering the same thing,' said Joe. 'They seem to *want* to go!'

It was only half an hour later, as they drew up to the entrance of Katz Castle, that Ginger began to lose the plot.

Ginger *hated* prison. He had spent half his last lifetime in one – paying his dues in a cramped, stinking 19th century cell – and then he'd had the misfortune to be reborn into yet another: a high-security cat's home. The very sight of this former prison brought up so many bad memories indeed, that he felt like Charles Bronson – the 'Tunnel King' in *The Great Escape*. Terror and claustrophobia gripped him, and he wanted out *right now*.

'Good grief!' said Joe, screeching to a stop. 'What's wrong with Ginger? He's gone flat as a pancake inside his cage and he's screaming like a demon!'

'Let's get him inside,' said Madge, grabbing Ginger's box and running up to reception. 'They'll know what to do!'

But they didn't. Ginger clapped eyes on Annie, his old nemesis, and let out such an unnatural howl – much like the one in *The Omen* – that she jumped back in fright and suggested he should go straight into quarantine.

'What are you *doing?*" Sparky called over to Ginger. '*Please* stop crying, or we'll never see each other again!

But it was to no avail. Ginger's blood was up and he wasn't listening.

Sparky then did the bravest thing in his young life. As soon as Joe turned up and let him out of his box, he ran quickly over to Ginger's and started pawing at it, crying in mock distress.

'Pretend like you're my best friend and calm down!' he hissed softly. 'It's our only chance...'

Ginger thought of Charles Bronson, and of how *he* had conquered his tunnel fears, and took the hint. He took a deep breath, thought of Barcelona, and went suddenly quiet.

'Oh, *that's* the problem!' said Annie as the two cats affectionately touched noses. 'They just want to be to-gether – how *cute!*'

And so, as Joe and Madge signed the admission regis-ter and left, Sparky and Ginger found themselves in the same cage.

'Phew, you were right,' complained Sparky, his nose wrinkling with disgust. 'Just one litter tray, and it stinks of other cats!'

'No time for that,' said Ginger with renewed compo-sure. 'We've only got seconds to get out of here, so just stick to the plan and don't fluff it.'

And with that he let out another Omen-like *'Whoooraow!'* – and sank his teeth into Sparky's neck. A chill ran down Annie's neck and she left her desk running. She dashed back into the main holding cell and viewed the scene there with alarm. The big orange one was apparently tearing the little black and white one to pieces! Without thinking, she tore open the cage door to attempt a rescue but was then bowled over by both cats bursting out at once and scampering to freedom. She never saw, but along the way Ginger darted into her office and sprayed generously on her mains plug. He hadn't wanted her using the phone.

Down at the driveway, Ginger was relieved to see Joe's van still there and the doors wide open. The two oomans were holding a map and were arguing over the best route to the airport.

'Quick!' he gestured to Sparky. 'Get in the back of the van and hide. And don't even squeak – they mustn't know we are here!'

Sparky was petrified, but he did as he was told. And as the van roared away from Faversham – a distraught Annie running vainly after it – four beings were on their way to Barcelona.

Chapter 7

The Road to Barcelona

A long hour later, Joe's battered old Transit rolled into Heathrow and came to rest in one of its labyrinthine multi-storey car parks.

As he reached forward to switch off the ignition, the last part of Ginger's cunning plan came into play and he spat a large fur-ball – one he had carefully prepared earlier – down Joe's neck. The sound of it being regurgitated was conveniently obscured by the last few revs of the dying engine.

'*Uurrrr!*' cried Joe, leaping out of the van and tearing off his shirt. 'What the heck was *that?*'

And in the confusion that followed, both cats made their getaway without being noticed.

'Well, that was the hard part,' said a satisfied Ginger. 'The next bit's easy-peasy!'

'Really?' said Sparky, gazing at the maze of twisting car-park concrete surrounding him. 'Where *are* we?'

'We're in Terminal One – I clocked it on the way in –

and Terminal One is where my mate Lee stops before he goes off to Spain.'

'You've got a *mate?*' said Sparky, quietly impressed. 'And he's going to be *here?*'

'Well, he's not really a mate, just an ooman wot talks a lot and gives me a free ride because I don't talk back. And I know he's gonna be here because it's a Sunday, and he *always* comes on a Sunday. He "knows" some-one, he says, and he picks up a few bottles of duty-free rum for his old dad in Portsmouth. His dad is *very* partial to the rum!'

Sparky's brow furrowed in puzzlement. They hadn't got to Barcelona yet and Ginger was already speaking in foreign tongues.

'Duty free? Rum? Portsmouth? You're frightening me. I want my humans back!'

'You'll see them soon enough,' said Ginger consolingly. 'But we got a deal, you and me, and I'd hate to see you break your word. Look, you're a good little pussy, you are, and I need you bad for this trip. I'm not just bringin' back a sombrero of grub this time. I'm going for the Full Monty – a whole *truck-load* of the stuff!"

'What *is* it with you and Spanish food?' sighed Sparky despairingly. 'You can get it right here in Surrey.'

'I is a *gour-met* cat,' said Ginger with a stubborn pout, 'and I don't want no imported rubbish. I want the *real thing* and I want it fresh off the table!'

Frank Kusy

'If you say so. But what are all these strange words you're using? What's "rum", for instance – and why do humans like it so much?'

Ginger gave a hollow laugh.

'Rum is like catnip to oomans. Well, some of them anyways. My old lady, the one wot adopted me, liked her rum. She drank it like water, and then she started singin' to herself and dancing around the carpet. After that, she just fell over. Sometimes on the sofa, sometimes on the floor, but she never made it to her bed. Poor ol' fing – rum was her only friend.'

Sparky's mind fled nervously to his kitchen back home. Was there any rum *there*? No, but he *had* seen ol' Joe pass out on the futon a lot lately. Was he drinking rum too? Or was it just his bad leg?

'You say you don't know much "ooman"', he accused Ginger, 'but you seem to have picked up an awful lot without telling me. You're just like ol' Joe with his missus – you can understand it when it suits you!'

'Oh, you noticed, did you?' chuckled Ginger, 'Well, I do have my moments. Most of the time though, I just can't be bovvered. Oomans don't generally interest me.'

Sparky rolled his eyes and sighed. 'Okay then, what's this "Portsmouth" place?'

'Oh, we have to go there to get the ferry,' smirked the orange cat. 'And before you say "wot's a ferry, then?" – because I know you just want to – it's a big metal fing, like ol' Joe's rubbish van, which takes us across the sea to Spain.'

'What's the sea?'

'Gawd, it's like talkin' to a *baby*. You don't know nuffink, do you? The "sea" is a bit like the pond at the end of your garden, but much, much bigger. And before you ask, there ain't no toads in it, so don't go looking – you won't find none.'

Sparky opened his mouth to ask yet another question, but Ginger was already on the move. He was sloping off down the car park in search of Lee's van. And because Lee was a creature of habit and always parked in the same spot, he found it at once.

'There you go!' he told Sparky with a satisfied grin. 'Regular as clockwork, is ol' Lee. We just gotta wait a bit, till he's done his bit of business, and then we're off to tapas land.'

'How do you know he'll like me?' asked Sparky timidly. 'He might leave me behind...'

'Wot? Lee? Of *corse* he'll like you! The more fings he gets to talk to – with all that borin' driving – the happier he is! All *you* gotta do is what you do best – look cute and down-trodden. And don't say nuffink. He likes to do *all* the talking.'

At that moment, a large man with ruddy cheeks and bright twinkly eyes appeared. It was Lee, and he recognised Ginger at once.

Frank Kusy

'*Allo* mate!' he greeted him cheerily. 'What are *you* doing here? I was only thinking the other day "where's that big fat ginger got to? He ain't been around for a while. Perhaps he's gone to meet his Maker!" And here you are, larger than life and just as ugly! Oh, and who's your little chum? He don't look too happy, do he, but he *does* have manners, sitting there all neat and polite like that. What's he doing with an old fart like you?'

Sparky rolled over in his very cutest pose and gave Lee an irresistible *prrrrrp!*

'See, he's a good un, I knew it. He's far too good for you, mate, he really is. Well, hop on board, the two of you, and let me tell you about my new carpet business...'

Lee was bored out of his skull with his present job. He had done it for four years now – trundling his huge Tesco's van full of English produce to supermarkets in Barcelona – and he badly wanted to give it up. He had never admitted this to his employers, but he had a severe case of claustrophobia and being cooped up in vans and ferries for four days each week (two on the way out, two more on the way back) made him want to hit things. As soon as he got out of his cramped little cab, he would punch walls, tables, even empty wheelchairs with old people only just out of them. That's why he liked cats so much. They calmed him down.

The other thing that Lee had a severe case of was verbal diarrhoea. He just couldn't stop talking. He even talked in his sleep, which was probably why he had never got married.

'Carpets,' he informed the two cats confidentially. 'I just can't get enough of carpets. The cleaner they get, the better I feel. Yeah, I know it's crazy, but I just can't help myself. I went round this house the other day – not far from where *you* hang out Ginger, actually – and there was this couple what had the most *horrible* carpets you ever did see. I turned up on their doorstep at 7am, which I know was a bit early but I was *keen* to start, and they wouldn't let me in – just threw three ratty rugs and a doormat at me and told me to "come back later." Well, those rugs didn't last long; I did them in about ten min-utes, so I filled in the time by ringing up this Irish biddy in Chiswick what keeps popping out babies. Gawd, she's got seven of them now and she's forever on the phone. "Lee, I've got this stain", she says, "the baby's knocked some-thing over!" I've got to the stage now, that I just spill stuff *myself!* If I'm short of a few quid, I just go over there, pour a cup of coffee on the carpet and blame it on the baby. She never notices, just glares at the kid and says "clumsy little clod!" Well, he can't talk back, can he? Mind you, he'll probably grow up to be a wrestler or a cage-fighter and do my head in. He'll *definitely* catch up with me one day!'

Ginger looked for Sparky, to tell him that Lee was *al-ways* like this – a hyped-up force of nature, constantly running at the mouth – but Sparky was hiding under the passenger seat, frozen with fear. Which suited Ginger just fine, since he could spread the entire bulk of his huge orange body right across the cosily padded double-seat.

Lee's next remarks had Sparky suddenly attentive.

'Yeah anyway, I returns to this first house – the one that turned me away earlier – and the same woman what chucked the rugs at me shouts back to her husband: "Joe, it's that Lee again, and he's brought enough hoses and cleaning fluid to sanitise Wembley Stadium!" And this Joe bloke totters up in his dressing gown and pyjamas, looking like some grumpy old hippy, and says "What are *you* doing here? I said noon, and here you are – back again – at ten am! *Tell* him, Madge, tell him what *noon* means!"

Joe? Madge? Sparky couldn't believe his ears. He stuck his head out from under the seat and, ignoring the roar of the lorry's loud engine, moved closer to hear more.

'..But I weren't being put off a second time,' continued Lee in his wide-boy Cockney accent. 'I told them – it's now or never, because I'm a busy man. And just *look* at those carpets. If I don't attend to them right away, they're going to just get up and walk! So I barge my way in, and the first thing this Joe geezer says is, 'I've just lost my cat. I'm going upstairs to chant for him!' Well, for

Ginger the Gangster Cat

some reason this tickles me. I'm a bit of a footie fan, I am, so I calls up to him, 'I thought you were getting ready for the Chelsea-Preston match, mate. Don't forget to chant for *Chelsea!*''

It was too much of a coincidence. Sparky looked up at Ginger, and Ginger looked down and smirked, 'Yeah, it's *you* he's talking about, you stoopid lost cat! And you was *lucky* you weren't in when Lee came calling. Because – take it from me – you can hear his bloomin' carpet machine a mile off. With your nerves, you'd have legged it a lot further than the bottom of your garden. You'd have been lost *forever!*'

'You two having a conversation?' said Lee, slightly irritated. 'Don't mind me. You miaow away all you like, I don't care. I just like the company. Now, where was I? Oh yes, when this Joe comes down again, I tell him: "Look at this, mate! I've done just one room, and there was so much gunk in it, I've had to use an extra bucket!" Well, I thought that would impress him, but it didn't. So then I *really* went to town and I didn't finish until the place was spotless. "You could make a *quilt* out of this, mate!" I said, pulling the last lumps of dead carpet out of my machine, and do you know what he said? He said "You *missed* a bit by the kitchen door." Ungrateful git!'

Two hours of inconsequential (but entertaining) chatter later, they finally rolled into Portsmouth and Lee leapt out of the cab. He casually swiped an innocent

71

dustbin, just to blow off some steam, and then he punched his own van - just to let it know how much he hated it.

'I'm going in to see my dad,' he informed the two cats. 'I'll be back in a jiffy.'

And with that, putting some water down for them and leaving both doors ajar, he sloped off down the road.

'Okay,' yawned Ginger, 'time for a poo! He knows I likes a poo in Portsmouth, does Lee. That's why he didn't lock us in.'

Sparky was horrified.

'You mean you're going to poo *outside?* He doesn't have a litter tray in *here*?'

'Oh, you are a one, ain't you?' chortled Ginger, having a good stretch. 'You ain't gonna see no litter tray for a long time to come, let alone poo in one. Either you follow me outside, or you can hold it all in until we gets to Barcelona!'

But Sparky wasn't going anywhere. He watched as Ginger leisurely left the vehicle and headed for some nearby woods. Peering through the window, he could just see Ginger's tail – way off in the distance – shivering with exertion, and it was then, quite suddenly, that he felt the same urge too.

With an instinct born of desperation, he climbed over the passenger seat and pushed his way – through another unlocked door – into the back of the well-stocked truck. And there he saw what he wanted immediately. A nice big bag of 'odour-free' cat litter.

He couldn't believe his luck. He tore the sack open with one paw, and scooped out a generous amount with the other. And then he sat down in the fresh fuller's earth and poo'd to his heart's delight.

After that, he mechanically scratched away at a nearby box, and discovered, to his further delight, that it contained some of his favourite cat food. He was just trying to work out how to open it when a familiar voice interrupted him.

'Wot you doin' back there?' hissed Ginger urgently. 'I got us a *mouse* to eat, so leave that ruddy processed stuff alone!'

But Sparky had tasted mouse once before and he hadn't liked it. He wanted proper cat food and nothing else. He managed to rip out one plastic pack from its box, and then he began biting and treading on it, hoping to squeeze out its contents.

'You're a stubborn little soldier, ain't you?' grunted Ginger. 'You look like some bloomin' Spanish grape-treader! Here, let *me* sort it out.' And with that he clambered clumsily to Sparky's side and sat heavily on the pack until it went 'pop!' and exploded.

'Being fat *does* have its advantages,' he informed Sparky casually, and then he returned to the front of the cab to torture his mildly protesting mouse.

Sparky had just finished eating and had rejoined Ginger, when the van door suddenly swung open and there was Lee again, his wild mass of greying curls framing the back of his head and looking more than ever like Coco the Clown.

'Cor!' he exclaimed loudly. 'Something don't half *niff* in here! Smells like the worst kind of cleaning fluid!'

Ginger rolled his eyes despairingly at Sparky.

'Don't tell me,' he said. 'You had a poo back there, didn't you? You just couldn't help yourself. And now we've got to live with it for the rest of the trip!'

Sparky crept fearfully back under the passenger seat. He had been a bad boy, a *very* bad boy, and if there had been a hole in the floor, he would have happily fallen into it. He was that embarrassed.

But he was lucky. Lee had a poor sense of smell, much poorer than cats, and besides, his nose was still stuffed up from a cold. He was also a bit tipsy, having just shared some rum with his dad, and was in a merry mood - chattering away to himself, oblivious to all else.

'Pity my dad's allergic to cats,' he commented happily. 'Because you'd have just *loved* this one. You know what he said? He said: "Me and the old duchess – that's what he calls me mum, y'know – have been married for *fifty years*. Blow me, I could have killed two people, got two life sentences, and have been *out* by now!"

Lee would have liked to say more, but he was now

nearing the ferry point and had to bundle both cats into the back of the van.

'Sorry, lads,' he apologised. 'But you know the drill, Ginger. No cats allowed on board, so you keep your pretty little chum *quiet* back there, okay? We don't want no customs geezers sniffing about!'

'Charming,' Ginger addressed Sparky. 'Now I get to sit in your stinky poo-place for the next 24 hours. Gawd, it *reeks* in here. Wot did you eat last night, curry?'

Sparky was still mortified. He tried to cover up his mess with yet more earthy litter, but this one was not as 'odour-free' as it claimed. With no ventilation shafts to let in fresh air, the whole storage area now stunk of tuna-flavoured botty burps.

'Well,' grunted Ginger, 'if you can't beat 'em, join 'em,' and he added a pile of his own poo to the mix.

'I didn't really let *go* in the woods,' he explained with a shrug. 'I had to catch that mouse in "mid flow".'

Sparky knew what Ginger was doing. He was trying to put him at ease. And that was the first time he knew that Ginger had feelings for him. He couldn't think of anyone else, even ol' Joe, who would have *poo'd* for him.

But he did have one last question.

'Why are we back here?' he asked timidly. 'Why can't we go up and see the sea?'

'Well, it's delicate like,' said Ginger, choosing his words with care. 'Some oomans fink we're not hygienic –

wot is ridick'lus because we clean ourselves much more than *they* do – and they don't want us invading Spain with fleas n' stuff!'

'Hasn't Spain got fleas, then?'

'Oh yeah, plenty of them. They even got a *song* about 'em called "Spanish Flea." But they don't want no more, so we gotta stay put. Besides, if we poke our heads out, Lee might lose his job. And that'd be curtains for my big plan...'

Sparky nodded in apparent understanding, and laid down to rest.

*

The lorry lurched aboard the ferry without event. The customs officials were so distracted by Lee's booming bonhomie that they completely forgot to search his vehicle.

Once aboard, surrounded by lots of other delivery vans in the hold, Lee made a hasty getaway. Just looking at them put him in the mood for murder.

'Where's he gone?' enquired Sparky hesitantly.

'Don't know, don't care,' grunted Ginger, climbing into the driver's compartment. "I'm goin' for a stroll. You coming?'

Sparky shook his head. The violent lurch of the ferry as it left its moorings had left him quite dizzy.

'Suit yourself. But I may be a while. I know this boat, I do, and I stashed away some rum on me last trip.'

Ginger the Gangster Cat

'Rum? I thought you said it was a bad thing.'

'Nah, I said it was bad for *oomans*. Especially the sad ones who've got nuffink else to live for. Me, I *loves* a tot of rum. Steadies my nerves, like.'

Sparky eyed him with suspicion.

'Nerves? I've never seen you nervous.'

Ginger hesitated. He was about to say it was the sea that made him nervous – that he had lost one of his previous lives to the rolling waves – but then he thought better of it. Sparky would think he was bonkers. He also didn't mention the (large) part that rum had played in his earlier demise. Sparky wouldn't have understood that either.

Instead, he gave a non-committal shrug and struggled out of the van through the open passenger window.

He was gone a long time.

*

Sparky was quietly dozing on a sack of dry porridge when he heard the noise.

"Sixteen kitties on an ooman's chest!

Yo, ho, ho, and a bottle of rum!"

It was a ghostly, drunken voice, and it came from outside the van.

Sparky shook himself awake, looked out the window, and saw Ginger propped up against one of the lifeboats. He had a funny scarf on his head, and a patch over one eye, and he could barely stand up.

Frank Kusy

'Oo's that?" croaked Ginger loudly. 'Billy Bones? Peg-leg Silver? Nah (hic), it's me ol' mate Sparky, innit? Bes' cat wot ever lived!'

'Are you all right?' whispered Sparky quietly.

'*Corse* I'm all right! "*Drink up, me hearties, and the devil has done for the rest!*" 'Ere, have some of this grog and sing along: "*Yo, ho, ho, a pirate's life for me!*"

'No, thank you. And what's that thing on your eye – can't you see?'

Ginger's face twisted into an evil leer.

'Rotten parrot! I told it to shut up, perched there on Long John's shoulder, but it wouldn't (hic) listen. "*Pieces of eight! Pieces of eight!* " it kept screamin', so I tried to take it out. How was I to know it was quicker than me? Stoopid bird – took my *eye* out instead!'

Sparky was getting worried. He had no idea what his crazy friend was talking about, but he knew one thing for certain – one more sea shanty, one more chorus of caterwauling nonsense, and he would never see his litter tray again. So he jumped on the door release, opened it out, and dragged Ginger in by the scruff of his neck.

It was not a moment too soon. The rum-sodden renegade had run out of song – and out of sea-legs too – and was collapsed in a sentimental heap around Lee's gearstick.

'No-one understans' me', he sobbed into his dampening eye-patch. 'You'se the only one, Sparky. You'se the only one...'

*

A long night later, Lee flung open the back of the van and said, 'Okay mateys, we're back on dry land. Time to stretch your legs...'

Sparky yawned and clambered out into the daylight.

'Where are we *now?*'' he asked Ginger.

'We're in Santander – sunny Spain,' yawned his orange friend, squinting thick-headedly at the sun. 'But we're not yet in Barcelona. That's a long way down the line, in Catalonia. Or, as the Spanish say, Catalunya. And no, don't ask, Catalunya ain't a place for loony cats. It just has a cat-like name.'

But then, after everything had gone so smoothly, they hit a snag.

Poor Lee had been sea-sick on the ferry – courtesy of a very large Sunday roast dinner – and he did not want to go back inside his van. He was feeling nauseous and could not face six more hours of intense claustrophobia.

'Sorry, pussies – I'm sick as a parrot,' he groaned miserably. 'If I have to drive again, I'm gonna just *hurl!*'

Ginger hadn't counted on this. He knew Lee was stupid, but not *that* stupid. Rum and roast dinners and rolling seas? What was he *thinking* ? He should have stuck to just the rum. Ginger shook his bleary head in annoyance. All of his grand schemes depended on this silly ooman, and he was falling apart before their very eyes.

It was then, quite unexpectedly, that Sparky saved the day.

He picked up a pen from the dashboard and wrote, in very spidery script,

Please tell us more about carpits

He inscribed it with the pen gripped tightly between his tiny baby-teeth, and he chose Lee's trousered left knee-cap as his message board.

'Blimey!' exclaimed Lee, shaken out of his malaise. 'How'd you learn to do *that?*"

Sparky had learnt to do that by studying the shopping lists ol' Joe had been issued by his missus. He had begun by scratching out the words 'sardines' and 'pilchards' – two cat foods he absolutely hated – and scrawling in the words 'chicken' and 'tuna' instead. Joe never noticed. Joe never noticed anything. He just went shopping and got what Sparky had cleverly re-ordered. After that, Sparky had moved on to bigger things. He had picked up more words from watching 'deaf' language on TV – words which appeared on the screen for humans whose ears did not work. And every so often, when he put together the spoken word and the printed words below, he would pick up a pen and write them down in a secret pad. He didn't know why or how he did this, but his earlier nightmare – where he'd been dying in the road – had not been a one-off.

He now had a recurring dream that he had been a

human in a past life, a learned human, and that his dearest wish – in that existence – had been to be come back as a cat.

But now he *was* a cat, he wasn't so sure. Something, some basic instinct, told him that nobody was interested in an educated cat. Either that, or they would become *too* interested, and he would be taken away for scientific experiments. He had seen *that* on TV too – the way that super-intelligent chimpanzees had been wired up, cut open, or even sent into space. And so, very wisely, he had kept his secret to himself.

Until, that is, right now.

Now he had no choice. He *had* to get Lee moving – by any means possible – or they would be stranded here forever.

And it worked.

Rejuvenated at having a feline *wunderkind* on his hands, Lee stared at the miraculous words on his kneecap, leapt into his cab, and did as he was told. He started talking about carpets again.

'Some people,' he confided joyfully, 'are real paranoid about their carpets. I had this one old biddy last week, and she was so terrified about what her neighbours might think, that she locked herself upstairs in her bedroom. Her carpets were so disgusting, I seriously thought she might top herself. "Where have you been?" I said when I eventually found her, and she said, "I've been sitting up here, thinking about that dirty water". And I said, "There *is* other things you can think about, love!'

From carpets, Lee moved onto his second favourite topic – vegetarians.

'There's nothing worse than vegetarians,' he informed the two cats. 'They don't look *well*, do they? All pasty-like and anaemic, and clinging onto tables for support. They could all do with a nice big juicy steak!'

Ginger nodded silent agreement. He couldn't argue with Lee there.

Only one thing was worse than vegetarians, in Lee's opinion, and that was vegans.

'Vegans!' he snorted dismissively. 'What are *they* all about? They put two fingers in a V shape, and then they start lecturing me about fish and cheese. As if I bloomin' care! My Grandad is 90 years old and has been living on a diet of pork crackling and dripping all that time, and he's happy as Larry!'

Ginger listened on, glad to be on the move again, but simply dying to ask Sparky one question.

His opportunity came soon, when Lee – inspired by his own talk about non-veg cuisine – stopped off at a roadside kiosk for a meat-stuffed taco.

'Okay, you sneaky little pussy!' Ginger accused Sparky. 'Wot's with you and this ooman *writing* lark? I've known you a long time, and I never saw you with a pen in your gob before!'

Ginger the Gangster Cat

'Do you believe in reincarnation?' asked Sparky quietly.

'Re-incarnate what?' sneered Ginger, secretly alarmed. 'Don't hit me with those big ooman words, or I'll re-incarnate *you!"*

'I have these dreams,' confessed Sparky. 'And in them, I am a very small human who ran into the road one day and got killed by a horse carriage. That's why I'm so *frightened* all the time. I'm scared that if I leave my kitchen, I'm going to die again.'

'That's ridik'lus!' scoffed Ginger. 'You're just imagining it!'

Ginger had put aside his own dreams of past lives. He hadn't liked the eye-patch.

'No, I'm quite sure,' said Sparky firmly. 'I've been getting a *lot* of these dreams lately, and in them I'm this little girl called Alice who is very good with words but is very bad at looking at the traffic. One day, she is so careless when crossing the road, she gets knocked over.'

'You're bonkers, you are! All I dreams about is little squirmy fings wot I chase around the garden and kill. That's wot *normal* cats dream about!'

'Well, I'm not normal then, am I?'

'But you can read *and* write ooman?' said Ginger, mystified. 'Is that why you watch so much TV?'

Sparky gave him a nervous nod.

'Well, you had me fooled. Me, I *hates* TV. I like the radio instead. Especially that Delia Smith ooman on Tuesday afternoons. "Recipes for Cats" – now that's what I *call* entertainment. I like Delia *lots,* because she talks non-stop about cat food! ' ...'Ere, I've just had a thought. Could you write her a letter from me?'

'What kind of letter?'

'Well, sumfink snappy like: "Dear Delia. Please come over and fill my fridge with every recipe possible. Here are your instructions on how I like to eat it: Open fridge. Empty contents onto floor. *Don't cook it*. I can't wait. Leave it *on* the floor. Lock the door on your way out."'

Sparky sighed. He knew he shouldn't have told Ginger his little secret. But it was too late now. Once they were in Barcelona, he knew, he would become his fat friend's pet monkey – a feline freak-show with infinite possibilities. He could just imagine himself writing 'Thank You' notes to every person who gave them food. And then they would want autographs, wouldn't they, and someone would come along and put him in a laboratory, and he would never see his humans again.

Once again, Sparky was a pussy in peril.

Chapter 8

Cats in Catalonia

Lee dropped them off at Ginger's favourite stomping ground – Las Ramblas, the main tourist drag of Barcelona. He was sorry to see them go, but he had deliveries to make. Deliveries which, unbeknown to him, would be turned away because they stank of cat poo.

Before they parted, he disabled a passing fruit trolley (well, he had to hit *something)* and left Sparky a little farewell note. It said simply: 'Be back here tomorrow noon. We can talk more carpets. I'll run you back to Surrey.'

Then, all of a sudden, he was gone and the two cats found themselves in a madhouse. Strange foreign smells and sounds filled the air, and the whole place was seething with loud tourists – mainly half-naked English lager-louts – and cunning little thieves out to fleece them.

'See that?' Ginger nudged Sparky. 'Those local kids just kick the visiting oomans in the shins, and when they bend down to rub them, they nick all the money out of their back pockets!'

'What's money?'

'Oh, you may be the Einstein of the pussy kingdom, but you've got a LOT to learn about things wot really *matter!*' said Ginger with a leer. 'Money is *everyfink* in the ooman world. How do you fink ol' Joe gets your food and your litter? He has to go down the supermarket and give them bits of dirty paper called "money" and if he hasn't got none, they don't give him anyfink. And it's the same right here. *We* haven't got no money, so no-one's going to give us anyfink either. We're goin' to have to make our *own* luck.'

'Luck?'

'Well, they don't fink much of cats, these Spanish oomans, so we're going to need lots of luck. And I've got a feeling - a very strong feeling - that you're luck on a stick!'

Sparky gave an inner groan. He didn't feel lucky at all. He just felt used.

He also felt very nervous. All these people, all that traffic, was making him very jumpy. In his mind, his worst nightmare was about to come true. He was going to get run over again and die and come back as what next? A limbless toad?

But Ginger was quite determined. The sun was now high in the sky, and he was in a hurry.

'This Barcelona lot,' he informed his frightened friend,

'has their feed time quite early. They eat until they burst, and then they go home – for wot they call a 'siesta' – and sleep it all off. It's too hot, y'see, for them to work or do fings in the daytime. So we've got to work fast, before they all keel over and stop givin' us stuff. And they won't give us stuff unless we give them sumfink to put it *in*...So 'ere's our first stop – right here.'

The "right here" was a tourist shop, just off the Las Ramblas, which sold (amongst other things) sombreros.

'We're gonna need a *lot* of these,' Ginger informed Sparky. 'So you go talk to the owner – yeah, do your sad pathetic thing – while I go ahead and nick 'em!'

'You're going to steal a heap of sombreros?'

'Well, I can't *pay* for them, can I? And I can't lift them on my own, so you got to keep that bloke busy for at least two minutes.'

Sparky walked forward, wondering what on earth he was doing, and looked up at the fat greasy Spaniard manning the shop. The Spaniard was called Pedro, and he didn't like cats. Pedro was indeed famous for not liking cats. If he had his way, he would be making sombreros *out* of cats.

But Pedro had not come across a cat like Sparky. Those big soulful eyes, that shivering little body, that unbearably plaintive little *prrrrrp!* It was all too much for poor Pedro. It was all he could do not to pick Sparky up and take him home and adopt him.

'*Que gato mas bonito!*' (What a cute cat!) he cooed, oblivious to the fact that Ginger was dragging away a large pile of sun-hats, '*Como te llamas?*' (What's your name, then?)

Sparky let himself be picked up and fussed over, and then he jumped down again – repelled by Pedro's over-powering reek of garlic – to rejoin a happy Ginger.

'Look at this lot!' exclaimed his fat orange friend, dragging his illegal haul of sombreros round the corner. 'We've got enough 'ere to keep us busy for *days!*'

But it didn't take days. It didn't even take an hour.

Ginger parked Sparky outside his favourite cafe, the Rita Rouge just behind the bustling La Boqueria, and gave him his instructions.

'Look,' he said. 'I've scored 'ere in the past – mainly by bitin' oomans in the leg and makin' 'em drop their food – so *you* should have no problem. Just...'

'Hang on,' interrupted Sparky. 'That sausage and pa-ella you gave me back in Surrey. You picked it off the *road?*'

'Corse I did!' snorted Ginger. 'Mind you, I did lick it clean first...'

Sparky shook his head in wonderment. It was a mira-cle he hadn't got food poisoning.

'Just sit *here*,' commanded Ginger. 'And go into your act. I'll be close by, and as soon as you fill up one som-brero, I'll be back to give you anuvver.'

Ginger the Gangster Cat

Sparky didn't know what was expected of him, but he did his best. He just sat there, looking sad and forlorn, and stared into an empty sombrero. It was enough. Sympathetic diners went 'Oh, pobrecito!'' or 'aaah, poor thing!' and began tossing things into his hat — squid rings, sausages, bits of fish and paella, and, every so often, a big juicy gamba prawn.

Sparky lifted his head with each new offering to give a pathetic little *prrrrrp!* And to speed things up, since he was now enjoying the attention, he picked up a nearby piece of chalk in his teeth and scrawled *my name's Sparky - what's yours?* on the pavement.

Well, that got them going. As Ginger had earlier predicted, people began simply *throwing* food at him — even locals who couldn't read English. It was the best circus trick they had ever seen, and they all wanted more.

I'm lost and hungry, he scribbled awkwardly, *thank you very much*

The deluge of food defeated even Ginger. He was so busy dragging away full sombreros and substituting empty ones, that he nearly had a stroke.

'Golly!' said Sparky when the crowd finally dispersed, 'twenty sombreros full of food. And all in just one lunchtime. Where are we going to *put* it all?

'I'm not stoopid,' puffed Ginger wheezily. 'I didn't tell you this, but I didn't eat that mouse earlier. I put it in Lee's freezer. Yeah, the big hummin' fing at the back of his van. And who's gonna fill a freezer with a dead mouse in it? Nobody. Especially not Tesco's, wot is so squeaky-clean and planet-friendly. They're gonna empty that freezer and *leave* it empty, in case they gets done by the law. Which means it's *our* freezer now, and we get to go home with all this lovely grub without it goin' off. Brilliant, eh?'

'Not so brilliant for poor Lee,' said Sparky sourly. 'Won't he lose his job or something?'

'He *hates* his job, does poor Lee!' retorted Ginger. 'He said so himself! He wants to do carpets instead. So we're doin' him a favour, right?'

'I suppose so,' said Sparky uneasily. 'But where *is* Lee's van? And how are we going to get all these sombreros into his freezer without him noticing?'

'Ah, that's where Sergei comes in...'

'Sergei?'

'Yeah, he's annuver "mate" of mine. He's a poor Polish plumber wot lives in a cardboard box nearby. You wait here, and I'll go fetch him.'

And with that Ginger waddled away, a stray chorizo sausage dangling from his whiskers and his tight, fat tummy scraping heavily against the pavement.

*

All was quiet. Siesta-time had kicked in and nobody was on the streets. The heat had reached boiling point and even the supermarkets were closed.

Ginger the Gangster Cat

Sparky felt weary too. Not just from the sun, but from all the recent excitement. He dragged himself into the cool shelter of a nearby car park, and with nothing to disturb him, fell into a deep but restless sleep.

Minutes passed, and Alice was back. The little girl of his dreams. And in this dream, she was in a large house - a Victorian mansion – and stroking her only friend, her pussycat Ralph.

'Oh, I'm so sad and lonely,' she was telling him. 'Thank heavens I have you.'

Ralph rubbed his head against Alice's knee and purred. She smiled, despite her tears. She was lucky to have such a faithful cat, with his glossy tortoiseshell fur and uncanny ability to understand her. And lucky to have a kind nanny who risked her father's fury every time she smuggled Ralph to her room just when she needed him most.

Like right now. Mama and Papa were arguing again and it sounded worse than the other times. Papa was shouting so loudly, even the servants would hear!

'If you are unable to discipline the staff,' he was raging, 'how can you control and train the child? You need to be *forceful*, Emily! I am writing to my unmarried aunt. She will reside as part of my household, in the room next door to the child. You may carry out your duties as usual, but Aunt Clarissa will be here to correct your mistakes and report your progress to me!'

Trying to block out the awful words, Alice held Ralph tight. 'I wish I was you,' she whispered. 'I wish I had someone to cuddle me and read *me* stories. I'd feel *so* much better then!'

An idea flashed through her mind. Of course! The new book that Mama had bought.

Excited now, Alice grabbed the book from beside her bed and sat cross-legged next to Ralph. She smiled as the cat peered at it, his head on one side as if he really was reading it.

'Alice in Wonderland' she declared. 'Yes, Alice, like me! It's about a little girl who meets with a big Cheshire cat. The cat is the only thing in the story that listens to her, like you, and it teaches her the rules of Wonderland. It tells her that she is mad for going there, that he is mad for being there, and that everyone in her imagined world is mad. It also disappears when it likes, leaving behind only its grin. I wish *I* could disappear like that – it would be *so* nice...'

She flicked through the pages and found the picture of the Cheshire cat beaming at the story-book Alice. 'Here we are. I'll do the voice of the cat all "purry" - like yours would be if you could talk.'

Ralph settled into her lap and Alice cleared her throat, ready to project her voice like her elocution teacher had taught her. Then she began. *'Would you tell me please, which way I ought to go from here...'*

Ginger the Gangster Cat

But the shouting downstairs was getting louder. *Crash!* Then a scream. Then silence.

'Mama!' Alice cried, jumping up and rushing to the door. She reached the balcony and looked down into the entrance hall. Her red-faced father was holding the door open and she glimpsed a flash of her mother's bonnet. She was leaving.

Alice raced down the stairs, past her flustered nanny and past the footman by the hat stand. Finally, she dodged around her father and ran into the street. She had only one thing on her mind – to catch up with her mother and go with her.

Alice didn't see the approaching hansom carriage. It bore down on her as she gave chase down the road, and in one unguarded moment, she slipped and fell under its wheels.

Her wish was fulfilled.

Just like the Cheshire cat, she faded away...

Chapter 9

Return of the Gangster Cats

Sparky woke up with a jump.

Ginger was back, and he had the strangest little man with him.

'This is Sergei,' he told Sparky. 'And you're gonna tell him how to help us.'

Sergei was a skinny little Pole with wild sticky-out hair, an even wilder bushy-browed stare, and a long hawkish nose. Sergei had been in Barcelona for close on a year, and was still looking for work. He was a plumber, a very bad plumber, and he had come here with just one ambition – to go to England and become a reality TV rock-star. It was a dream he had had since childhood, and he practised on a battered old karaoke machine – discovered in a lonely dumpster – each and every night. His favourite song was *Thriller* by Michael Jackson, and he liked to en-act it, with thrusting dance moves thrown in, outside crowded restaurants. It was an alarming sight, and also his only source of income, since trapped diners often paid him to go somewhere else.

Sergei had two problems. First, he couldn't get to England, because he didn't have a work permit. Second, he had very little English – just a smattering of odd phrases (gleaned from a pre-war phrase-book) like 'Top Notch!' and 'Steady on, old boy!' Along, of course, with a few slang expressions he had picked up from British tourists. His favourite slang expression at present was '*Bite* me!' – which had a nice ring to it, but for some strange reason had rarely gone down well with locals. Neither had the two euro ad he had posted in Cafe E Canto, his local bar, which said simply, 'My name Sergei – I fix you *good!*' The extra one euro to explain this was currently beyond his means.

'My friend bring me good sausage,' gasped Sergei, all hot and sweaty after following Ginger down the heat-blasted pavement. 'What is problem?'

Sparky pointed one paw at the mountain of food before him, and with the other, he put the chalk back in his mouth and scrawled *how big is your box?* on the ground.

Sergei was entranced. He had never come across a literate cat before, and he was in awe. He was especially in awe that this little pussycat could write better English than himself.

'Is BIG box!' he stammered in astonishment. 'Why you need?'

Sparky went into a quick huddle with Ginger, and then wrote: *please bring box here and put all this food in it – take us to Tesco's*

'Grupo Tesco in Solanes street?' said Sergei. 'That is very long way, three mile or more. And I like my box very much. It is my home. Why I give it you?'

Ginger gave Sparky an urgent whisper. 'Tell him what he wants to hear. Tell him we're taking him to England!'

Sparky was running out of chalk, but he conveyed the message.

'You take me to the *England?*' beamed Sergei eagerly. 'Well, *bite* me! I am so happy!'

And with that he ran off, his scrawny little form darting back up the tarmac like a deranged hobbit.

'Why did we have to lie to him?' said Sparky, crossly. 'Lee is never going to smuggle him into Surrey.'

'Lee is not *going* to Surrey,' replied Ginger. 'We're nicking his van.'

'What?'

'Yeah, I've already nicked his passport, and all we gotta do is put Sergei's photo in it instead. We'll get *that* from Sergei's passport.'

'So who's going to drive? Sergei?'

'Well, he does speak funny-like, but I heard him say once that he drove a tractor back in Poland. So a Tesco's lorry should be *no* problem!'

'You are one disturbed cat,' said Sparky, quietly. 'I

think I had a dream about you just now, and it wasn't good.'

'Oh yeah?'

'It was in the olden days and you were a really bad lot. I was a little girl called Alice who died, and her precious cat Ralph went looking for her, and he found *you* instead.'

'And I smothered him with hugs and kisses?'

'No, you didn't. You used him to beg and steal food for you.

'Wot was I, then? A furry Fagin?'

'Yes, something like that. Anyway, you used to make poor Ralph steal – sausages mainly – from the poor and the sick and then you took them all off of him.'

'Well,' quipped Ginger, 'yer gotta nick a sausage or two!'

'No wonder he reported you to the police,' said Sparky.

'Oh, did he? I don't remember that.'

'Yes, you probably do. That's why you've got it for ol' Joe, isn't it? Even when you chased him – or rather, Ralph – into the forest and left him to die.'

'I never!'

'It wasn't nice,' said Sparky decisively. 'The more I think about it, the more I want to go home.'

'Nah, you can't do *that!*' panicked Ginger. 'It was just a dream, weren't it? You could have got it wrong. Besides, we've come too far to turn back now! Think about it. Everybody gets wot they *want* – we get our grub home safe, Sergei goes to Surrey and becomes a poncy rock star, and Lee, well, he gets a nice holiday in sunny Spain.'

'You've got it all worked out, haven't you? Except the parts about getting *to* Tesco's and getting all this food into a locked van.'

'Locked?' snickered Ginger, with a knowing wink. 'It ain't never *been* locked. Lee is so keen to get rid of it, he never locks up. He even leaves the keys in the ignition, hopin' that someone will drive it away. And as for getting to Tesco's, well, I ain't exactly worked that one out yet, but Sergei will think of sumfink. He's so keen on England, he'll probably *carry* it there!'

'What, three miles? I don't *think* so. Look at him – here he comes now – and that box is even bigger than he is!'

Sergei arrived, dripping with sweat but triumphant. The crumpled cardboard box, folded up for carrying ease, unfurled into an enormous container six feet high.

'I am good *egg!*'' he declared proudly. 'Bring home the *bacon!*"

And without further ado, he scooped up the pile of heaped sombreros and emptied their contents into his ex-domicile.

'Now is peachy-dandy!' he announced. 'What *next*

do?"

Ginger had been thinking about this, and there was only one solution. It was obvious, even to him, that Sparky was right. The box was now so full of food that Sergei would not even be able to lift it, let alone drag it, three miles up the road.

Ginger's solution was simple. If they could not get to Tesco's, then Tesco's – in a manner of speaking – would have to come to *them.*

He went into another quick huddle with Sparky and made him write one last message.

Please drive us to England. We have new passport for you – also big van. Take me to Tesco's then come back – Ginger guard food.

Sergei flicked desperately through his well-thumbed English phrase-book. He thought he understood what Sparky was saying, but he couldn't be sure.

'Ah *ha!*' he said at last. 'Ginger cat stay here. You go with me. *Top notch* idea!'

*

But if Ginger thought he had it easy, sitting in his cardboard fortress of gourmet food, he was wrong.

As soon as Sergei and Sparky had left, he heard a familiar voice.

'Ere, amigo,' it said, 'Giss'us a prawn!'

Ginger's head whipped round and he saw a face from

the past.

'Blimey!' he stuttered. 'Scampi, isn't it? Wot's an old lag like *you* doin' here? I ain't seen you for *ages!*"

'It's not Scampi anymore,' retorted the big, black tom-cat. 'It's "Miguel" now and don't you forget it! And what am I doing here? I'm doing what every other stray cat is going to be doing in a minute - sniffing that lovely, big box of goodies you're sitting on and wanting some of it. You need protection, mate, and I'm here to give it you!'

Ginger and Scampi went way back.

Back to the time they had led a sixteen-strong pussy posse (in a former life) on a crime spree that had been the talk of Victorian London.

And more recently, to the time they had shared a cage at Annie's Katz Castle and had beaten each other to a pulp. On this occasion, just before Ginger had been moved to isolation, they had become uneasy chums and had agreed to meet up on the outside. It had been Scampi who had first put Ginger onto Barcelona. He had taken him there one day, in a Sainsbury's lorry, and had shown him the wonders of authentic Spanish cuisine. In return, he had used Ginger as his main 'hit man' – the cat most likely to inflict pain on any other strays who invaded their patch.

But now it was Ginger who needed *his* help, not the other way round.

'I know you,' said Ginger, cautiously. 'And you don't

want one prawn. You want your usual "cut".'

Miguel shrugged.

'Look, I just broke out sixteen hungry moggies from a ruddy cats' home and I ain't got time for no bargaining. Fifty-fifty. Take it or leave it.'

'Gotta leave it, mate,' said Ginger. 'There's a third party to fink about – a little guy called Sparky – and I didn't get all this grub myself. He did most of the work.'

Miguel looked over his shoulder, and then back at Ginger. As the sun reached its zenith, and the delightful aroma of free Catalonian cuisine filled the air, a hungry legion of convict cats were gathering fast.

'Forty-sixty, mate. My last offer. I don't like this Spanish lot – they're thick as planks and they don't speak the Queen's English – but this is my manor now and I want to keep it that way. You ain't gonna make it on your own...'

Ginger considered. Yes, he probably did need help – one look at the assembling horde told him that – but he hadn't lost a fight yet and he wasn't about to start.

'No dice, "Miguel" – or whatever you call yourself now. I can handle it.'

'Suit yourself,' sniggered Miguel and sat back to watch.

'Hola, Senor!' shouted up the lead gangster cat, scratching at the foot of the box. 'My name Felipe – remember *me*? *"Pieces of eight! Pieces of eight!"* Yes, I was the parrot-bird that take out your eye before, ha, ha!

And say hello to my little friends Pepe and Jose. They are happy to meet with you again also. Pepe, he was the eagle who eat you up in India, yum, yum, and Jose, he was your mama-*gato* one time, and leave you to drown!'

Ginger stared down with dawning recognition.

'Oh, so it's *you* lot again, is it? I should've known! But tell me this — why have you got it in for me? I've done nuffink to you!'

'"Nuffink?" echoed Felipe. 'Oh, *por favor,* big ginger cat, you remember not. You remember not the sixteen Christian humans you eat in the Roman arena? You are very *bad* ginger cat back then — very fat lion *gato.* We follow you like bad smelling thing — from one lifetime to the next — and we are no longer so Christian feeling. You must pay.'

'That's rich!' scoffed Ginger, looking around for a weapon and coming up with a dustbin lid. *'You're* the ones what want payback? I got your number in my last life, when you scarpered off to Spain and left me to rot in that horrible little cell! Not forgettin' the time when you all ganged up on me and had me blinded along with that dotty ol' witch. Wot was *her* crime, anyway? She was a good ooman, as it went.'

'Lion tamer!' called across Miguel. 'Didn't like Christians!'

Ginger reared up in his box, a scruffy, fat crusader ready to defend the Cross.

Ginger the Gangster Cat

'Well, *come* on then!' he roared. *'COME on!'*

Felipe hesitated. This was one bad-ass pussy cat, and he looked *very* upset.

'Tranquilo, grande gato! Please no angry! Give us food and we call it...how you say..."quits". It is fair, no? Before you eat us. Now, you feed us. *Enjoy* your last life. Do not make us kill you again.'

'It's a good deal,' chipped in Miguel. 'Take it, mate!'

But Ginger's blood was up. Eight long lifetimes of persecution now rankled in him and he hadn't deserved any of it. How was he to know that eating oomans was bad? Nobody had told him.

'I don't deal with *scum*!' he hollered down. 'Let's *BOOGIE!'*

And with that commenced a battle royal. There Ginger stood, a lone beleaguered warrior in a siege-tower of hoarded food, while rank upon rank of howling, spitting, cursing gangster cats set upon him and attacked his cardboard castle.

The first to go was Felipe. No sooner had he got to the top than he was smashed down again, sent flying by one mighty thrust of Ginger's dustbin lid.

'Mierda!' he cried, clutching one eye, 'I'm blind!'

'An eye for an eye!' chortled Ginger. 'Stoopid exparrot!'

Pepe and Jose were next – one batted for a six into a tree, the other held down in a full sombrero until he lost consciousness.

'That'll teach you, you reincarnated rotters!' raged Ginger. 'You've had your nine lives and now your time is up! No more sneaky eagles and bad mothers for *you!*'

But then he was swiped from behind — a dirty blow that took off an ear — and he fell crashing out of his tower of treats.

Miguel, who had been waiting patiently on the sidelines, watched him go down.

'I can't take it no more,' he muttered to himself. 'What's he trying to do, kill hisself?'

And with a loud, terrifying yowl he dashed into the fray, scraped a dozen crazed pussies off of Ginger, and hauled him back onto his box.

'There you go, matey,' he puffed. 'Call it thirty-seventy. I'm not greedy.'

Ginger had no time to reply. He was now assaulted on all sides, and he no longer had his dustbin lid. Miguel had his back, but he couldn't see his front. Blood from his severed ear was trickling into his eyes, and he was fighting blind.

'Good *Gawd!*' shouted Miguel as the box filled up with marauding moggies. 'It's like that ooman bloke Custer and his last stand against the Indians! Where's the bloomin' *cavalry*?'

As if on cue, the cavalry arrived. Or rather, a halting, juddering Tesco's van with Sergei at the wheel. The poor

Ginger the Gangster Cat

little Pole had not yet mastered the steering, and the van had three more gears than his old farming tractor. So he just ploughed it into the busy food mountain – scattering every gangster cat in sight – as he tried to find 'neutral.'

It was fortunate timing, since Ginger and Miguel had nearly been overwhelmed. The fight had left them battered and bruised, and they barely had breath left to speak.

'Well, you took your time,' croaked Ginger, wiping his eyes clear. 'Wot took you so long?'

'Oh, you're *hurt!*' cried Sparky, leaping forward to lick his damaged friend. 'What happened to your ear?'

'Same as the other one now – got a matching set. Wot *did* take you so long?'

'Sorry about that,' apologised Sparky, meekly. 'But Sergei hasn't driven for ten years. And he didn't even pass his tractor exam.'

'Is this your "third party"?' sneered Miguel, preening his sleek black fur. 'He don't look up to much. He's just a *baby!* Let's cut him out, mate. We did all the fighting!'

Ginger did not hesitate. He sank his teeth into Miguel's neck and flung him to and fro until he begged for mercy.

'You ain't my "mate", mate!' said Ginger, finally spitting Miguel out. '*Sparky* is my mate – my *only* mate – and you're just fodder for the ants. Here, take your ruddy prawn, you earned it, but that's all you're gonna get from me. Now, *adios* and get lost before I bust your bloomin' head!'

'What was that all about?' asked Sparky, as Miguel quietly slunk away. 'And am I really your only friend?'

'Well, I said it so I said it,' mumbled Ginger uncomfortably. 'No-one's gonna cut *you* out and get away with it. We had a deal, you and I, and you did me proud. So I guess that makes us pals for life. You got a *problem* with that?'

'No, no,' said Sparky, secretly pleased. 'No problem at all...'

Chapter 10

Surrey or Bust

The real problem arose as they finished loading the van. Yes, it was still working (incredibly) but then Sergei began reversing it back into the road. And as he did so, two figures came round the corner. Two figures who recognised their cats at once.

'Sparky? Ginger?' said Joe and Madge in unison. 'What are *you* doing here?'

'Oh Gawd!' Ginger groaned to himself. 'Now we're in for it!'

What he meant of course was that *he* was in for it. He knew he had taken a risk, that Joe and his missus were in town and he might just bump into them. But he had never expected to see them wandering around during the hottest part of the day.

Result? He was in poo up to his neck. They would never forgive him *this* time.

Sparky, on the other hand, was overcome with joy. He had never expected to see his humans either, not in this lifetime, and here they were, miraculously, standing right before him.

He sprang forth to greet them and leapt excitedly into Joe's arms. He dug his nose into the ageing hippy's face and then he leaned over to lick Madge's face as well. He was a cat in ecstasy and, no matter how hard he tried, he could not stop purring.

'Well, we missed you *too!*' said Joe, tears of sentiment welling up in his eyes. 'I knew we shouldn't have left you behind.'

'Yes,' cooed Madge soothingly. 'He's been talking about nothing else ever since we arrived. It's been "Sparky this" and "Sparky that", and "I wonder what *Sparky's* up to right now?" Well, we know now, don't we? That naughty Ginger's brought you all the way to Barcelona. Where *is* the evil old mog anyway?'

The 'evil old mog' had shot back into the van. He was a bad cat again, he knew it. Perhaps the worstest bad cat in the universe. And he wasn't coming out of that van in a hurry. He clung onto a surprised Sergei, still at the wheel, and hid his head in shame.

It was lucky for him – very lucky – that Sparky remembered their last exchange. The one where Ginger had suddenly, out of the blue, declared his undying friendship.

Having finished dripping saliva over his rediscovered humans, Sparky grabbed a marker pen from Joe's top pocket, leapt down to the ground again, and wrote a quick message on the side of the shiny-white van:

Dear ol' Joe it read. *Do you remember Alice?*

Joe's shock at seeing his cat with a pen in its mouth was overcome by his shock at the message itself.

Of *course* he remembered Alice. It was the main reason he had stopped going to bed lately. Every time he closed his eyes, there she was: the small bookish girl with the pen in *her* mouth. It had still been in her mouth when she was writing a story for her beloved cat Ralph, the day before she died.

'You're *"Alice?"* he declared with astonishment.

Yes and you're Ralph! wrote Sparky. *I'm SO happy to find you again!*

'Me too!' said Joe, grabbing back his baby cat and smothering him with kisses. 'I *knew* we'd met before! But I always thought you were my poor dead mum, not *Alice!* She's been giving me nightmares for weeks!'

'What about Ginger?' scoffed Madge, bringing them both back to reality, 'What was *he*? The Artful Dodger?'

Sparky was running out of van-space to write on, so he chose a low wall instead.

Ginger was a bad cat he wrote. *In my dreams he was a very bad cat – but now he is a very GOOD cat – he is my new best friend – you must not punish him!*

'Oh, and why's that then?' said Madge, still fascinated with Sparky's new-found literary talent. 'He's brought you all the way here, for his own selfish purposes, no doubt, and you want us to *forgive* him?'

It was then, as the wind suddenly changed direction, that the salty, flavoursome reek of seafood from the van hit her, and she dived inside to investigate.

'Just as I thought,' she called back to Joe. 'There's a whole freezer-full of messed-up Spanish scraps in here. *And* a telltale sombrero. If that's not Ginger's work, I don't know what is!'

Joe hobbled to the side of the van, to see who was manning it, and was greeted by a happily waving Sergei.

'Who the heck are *you?*' he demanded. 'And why are you trying to steal our cats?'

'Steady *on*, old boy!' said Sergei, the smile slowly draining from his face, 'My name Sergei and I am top-notch hoity-toity good egg. You no take Ginger cat. He is friend of mine. If you try to take, your ducks will come home to sit on the grill!'

'I think he means "our chickens will come home to roost!" Joe called to Madge. 'He's not coming out. What are we going to *do*?'

Madge had no idea what to do. All she knew was that she had two stubborn cats, an even more stubborn Pole, and a stinky white van on her hands. And this vexed her greatly. She had barely been in Barcelona a day and her carefully worked-out sightseeing schedule – prepared with typical Germanic zeal on the flight over – was falling apart.

'I don't know!' she wailed. 'Ask Sparky!'

But Sparky wasn't needed.

It was Sergei who saved the day.

Sensing that his long-awaited trip to England was in dire jeopardy, he leapt down from the cab with his karaoke machine and gave the surprised couple an impromptu performance of his favourite song – yes, *Thriller* again, and this time with no holds barred.

Joe and Madge watched on in amazement. It was quite the most bizarre spectacle they had ever witnessed. The flailing arms, the frenzied clapping, and the manic moon-walking were one thing. But the terrifying werewolf noises – like a madman baying at the moon – were quite another. A chill ran right up their spines and they wanted him to stop.

When he did finally stop, he made a quick bow and said, 'I like the Michaels Jacksons. I like to go England and be big star on *X-Factor*. What you think?'

Joe didn't know what to think, but he clapped politely and said, 'What about our cats?'

'No worry for cats!' replied Sergei. 'I am easy-pleaser. I take cats to England also!'

Joe and Madge exchanged a secret smile. Anyone this crazy, and this crazy about cats, might just make it.

'You're mad as a box of frogs, mate,' Joe informed him. 'But here – take these house keys, and some petrol money too, and be our cat-sitter for a week. You'll be doing us both a favour.'

Joe knew that Sergei didn't understand one word he had said, but that didn't matter. Sparky would interpret for him, and Ginger would give him directions. If only Sergei could avoid being arrested for bad driving, he should have them all back home by tomorrow.

'Nice one!' said Madge happily. '*Far* better than cancelling our trip and smuggling three illegal immigrants home by ferry. Now, let's get back to my itinerary. It's the Gothic area next – and you'll like this – a slap-up birthday meal at *Els Quatre Gatos.*'

'*Els* what?'

'The Four Cats. It's where Picasso and Gaudi used to hang out, and it's a whole lot better than two lost cats in a van or three stunned cats in a stupid cat zoo. I hear the chicken there is *divine!*'

'And how are we going to pay for that? We've still haven't got any euros.'

'Oh,' tittered Madge craftily, 'that's the one thing I *did* get right. I rang up ahead to book it, and I left my credit card details. We'll sort out the bill tomorrow.'

Joe picked Sparky up one last time.

'Gonna miss you "Alice", he said sadly. 'But it'll only be for a few days this time – not another lifetime.'

Sparky dug his head into Joe's greying beard and gave him his fondest farewell *prrrrp!*

'Yeah, I hear you, buddy. "Ralph" hears you. And no, I'm not going to break another leg and die in a forest. I'm going to get a good night's sleep for once – you too, I hope – and if we meet in dreams again, we are going to be together. We are *always* going to be together.'

Ginger leaned cautiously out of the cab window.

'Yeah, and I'll be there right *with* you!' he chuckled to himself. 'You ain't seen the last of *me!*'

THE END

About the author

FRANK KUSY is a rather fat Buddhist who likes playing bridge with little old ladies and writing silly stories about cats.

He wrote his first cat book when he was eight. It was called 'Jessie the Cat' and even his mum liked it. There followed 'Toad's Dilemma' (a sequel to Frank's all time fave kid's book, 'The Wind in the Willows') and a whole host of similarly derivative anthropomorphic master-pieces. Only after a short affair with journalism in his 20's did he write anything with a human being in it (the Financial Times insisted upon it), and only after he went to India, aged 30, did he stop writing about cats (he only saw one in India).

Frank's first published book (1986) was a travelogue

on India – to be re-released here on Grinning Bandits as *Kevin and I in India*. 'I wrote it to avoid having to return to a mind-numbing job in Social Services.' There followed a slew of Asian travel guides – India, Thailand, Burma, Indonesia etc – but none of them paid very much and the last one gave him a ten-year writing block: he simply couldn't decide which Delhi hotel had the best bathroom, the Taj Intercontinental or the Oberoi.

Frank returned to writing after breaking his leg in 2005 – his wife nagged him into it. And the first thing they penned together was...another cat book. Thus came into being 'Ginger the Gangster Cat', the story of one fat cat's devotion to Spanish cuisine. For anyone interested, Sparky – their 3-year old perennial kitten and Ginger's shy and nervous sidekick – is real. He really is the cutest cat in the universe. Ginger himself is a composite of every stray tom-cat Frank has had in the past, absolute terrors all of them!

Ginger the Buddha Cat

by Frank Kusy

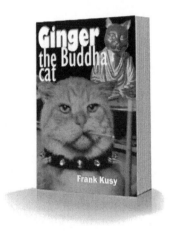

Ginger is back, and facing a tough decision. Sausages or enlightenment?

Ginger is about to relive the first of his nine lifetimes upon this earth - as a fat greedy god-cat in ancient India. With the help of his little pal Sparky, the cutest cat in the universe, he must curb his appetites and bring home the top sausage known to Man - without eating it.

   If he succeeds, he will win the heart of Madame Frou-Frou, the foxiest kitty on the block. He will also prove himself worthy of becoming the Buddha's cat. If he fails, no good cat will ever go to Heaven.

Can Ginger overcome his attachment to sausages? Can he really be bothered to save feline-kind? After 2000 years and nine horribly mis-spent lives, it doesn't seem likely...

GRINNING BANDIT BOOKS

A word from our sponsors …

If you enjoyed *Ginger the Gangster Cat*, please check out the sequel: *Ginger the Buddha Cat.*

And, for adults:

Rupee Millionaires , and Kevin and I in India – all by Frank Kusy (Grinning Bandit Books).

Weekend in Weighton by Terry Murphy (Grinning Bandit Books).

Scrapyard Blues by Derryl Flynn (Grinning Bandit Books).

The Ultimate Inferior Beings by Mark Roman (Cogwheel Press).

11042002R00072

Printed in Great Britain
by Amazon.co.uk, Ltd.,
Marston Gate.